The Wager

──────── *Also by Machado de Assis* ────────

Esau and Jacob
Yayá Garcia

Machado de Assis

THE WAGER

Aires' Journal

*Translated from the Portuguese
and with an Introduction by
R.L. Scott-Buccleuch*

PETER OWEN · LONDON

PETER OWEN PUBLISHERS
73 Kenway Road London SW5 ORE

Translated from the Portuguese *Memorial de Aires*.
First published in Great Britain 1990
English translation © Peter Owen Ltd 1990

British Library Cataloguing in Publication Data
Assis, Machado de, *1839–1908*
The wager   Aires' journal.
I. Title   II. Aires' journal
869.3'3

ISBN 0–7206–0772–8

Typeset by Selectmove London
Printed in Great Britain by Billings of Worcester

Introduction

Published in 1908, the year of his death, *The Wager* is the last of Machado de Assis's nine novels. Yet far from showing him in decline, it reveals him still at the height of his powers, and for many critics this work represents the full maturity of his art and thought. Here are to be found all the qualities of his former masterpieces, the shrewd observation of human behaviour, the keen wit, whimsical humour and gentle irony, now imbued with an autumnal sadness and resignation that seem to presage the end.

In contrast to his earlier novels, Machado de Assis presented *The Wager* in the form of a diary, and for this purpose resurrected a character introduced in *Esau and Jacob*, published four years earlier, the retired diplomat, José da Costa Marcondes Aires, whose journal is referred to in that book. In a brief foreword Machado de Assis explains that apart from omitting passages unrelated to the main story he transcribes the journal exactly as he found it, preserving the writer's own words and style. The result is an extraordinary degree of realism, as Aires corrects observations made previously and adds items he had forgotten to include. The entries too are sometimes in note form, making Machado de Assis's normal taut, deceptively simple style even more concise and even more of a challenge to the occasionally despairing translator. But the end result is a delight to those who have a true feeling for words, and consequently a love of this Brazilian master who, in an age more given to baroque pomposity, taught his countrymen how to use words to best effect.

As in other of Machado's novels the story is of secondary importance, the primary interest being in the characters themselves. Here, in *The Wager*, the story is virtually non-existent, unfolding itself in a leisurely manner as one entry follows another. Indeed, the inattentive reader may not be immediately aware that Aires's casual bet with his sister that Noronha's widow will remarry is the germ of the whole plot, so slowly does the action proceed. Yet the plot itself is merely incidental, a means to allow a delightful study of the Aguiars, the elderly couple who, if we omit the writer of the journal himself, are the main characters of the novel. In these two, many critics have seen a self-portrait of Machado and his wife, Carolina, who had died some years before. Undoubtedly there are many resemblances between Carolina and Dona Carmo, and it is certain that memories of his wife must have influenced the author, but apart from the coincidence of the initials – Carolina, Carmo; Assis, Aguiar – there seems little to connect the two men. Machado's voice is rather to be heard in that of Aires himself.

At this point perhaps a word of explanation is needed for modern readers who may be puzzled by the fact that Dona Carmo, a woman of only fifty, is portrayed as a frail old lady nearing the close of her life. Aires, though sixty-two, constantly refers to her as *a boa velha* – the dear old lady. It must be remembered that Brazilian girls have always tended to marry early, and until quite recently it was not uncommon for them to be wives and mothers at the age of twelve or thirteen. After regular child bearing they were middle-aged in their twenties, and by forty they were old women. Admittedly those of a stronger constitution might live on to a ripe old age, but the majority died young, leaving the husband free to take himself another child wife. Dona Carmo had no children, but women of her age were regarded as old and, more important, felt themselves to be so.

The story, such as it is, is centred on the elderly couple, their circle of friends, their 'adopted children', their hopes and fears and final crushing disappointment, all of which give ample scope for the author's shrewd, ironic observation. His canvas is a small one, but what it lacks in scope is more than compensated for by richness of detail. No one escapes his penetrating eye, not even Aires himself who, as an elderly man, and well aware of the figure he cuts, still allows himself to be tempted by the charms of the attractive young widow, Fidelia (whose name, whether attributable to Beethoven or not, is itself an example of Machado's gentle irony).

Like Sterne and Fielding, to whom he owed so much, Machado was accustomed to speak in his own voice in many of his novels, adding his own observations and comments on the actions and attitudes of his characters. In *The Wager* Aires is his spokesman, and since, as he says, he writes 'to my journal, for my journal', which is destined to be consigned to the flames, he has unlimited freedom of comment, and can even indulge in sly digs at himself. For Machado's purpose he is the ideal figure – a sexagenarian widower and former diplomat who, though he has lost all his illusions, still retains a deep-rooted love of his fellow men, fellow sufferers in an inexplicable world, whose tragedy can be borne only by refusing to take it too seriously.

In keeping with his character, this love of Aires's is implicit, rarely explicit, even in the private confidences made to his journal. More open and acknowledged, however, is his love of his native city, Rio de Janeiro, a love which is heightened by his return after a long absence, and by the awareness that at his age his period of renewed acquaintance will necessarily be short. Machado himself lived and worked all his life in Rio de Janeiro and, like most of the characters in his novels, rarely absented himself from it. Like Aires he was conscious of his own approaching end, a consciousness which adds poignancy to the few light touches he makes in praise of the city he knew and loved so well. Within a few months of writing *The Wager* Machado de Assis was dead.

In no other of his novels is the idea of death so constantly present. Appropriately enough the action begins in a cemetery, the heroine is a widow, and later deaths recorded in the journal affect the course of the courtship of Fidelia and Tristão. With the exception of the young lovers all the main characters are elderly, if not old, yet perhaps through the influence of a firm religious faith (not immediately apparent in Aires himself), they appear to have come to terms with their situation and accept death with a philosophical resignation reminiscent of Victorian England. The theme is acceptance, not revolt: the old have had their lives and must allow the young to lead theirs. So Aires himself comments when, at the end of the novel, the newly-weds sail away to begin a new life in Portugal, leaving their grief-stricken 'parents' to comfort each other in their lonely old age.

In many ways *The Wager* recalls a work of a very different nature, written a mere eleven years later. Elgar's Cello Concerto, though not his last composition, has about it the same air of finality, of sadness and resignation, of acceptance without despair. Both were written by old men who had retained all their earlier powers, and both are, in a way, a summing up of their life's work. Both men wrote during a period of sweeping change, and no doubt were conscious of that fact. Both works, in their different ways, depict a world and a way of life that exist no more, and by the time of their composition a new era had already begun. If Elgar draws a picture of the comfortable, colourful Edwardian England that died in the First World War, Machado shows us Rio de Janeiro on the eve of changes equally momentous. The abolition of slavery is actually recorded in *The Wager*, while the deposition of the Emperor Dom Pedro II and the proclamation of the Republic, a possibility mentioned, took place just a few months after the last entry. The contrast between the two worlds is vividly depicted in Aires's reflections during his trip up to Petropolis, when he contrasts the speed, comfort and boredom of the train journey with the leisurely, picturesque and sociable nature of the ascent by mule train. The old relationship of masters and slaves is a further point in question. But Machado's horizons are deliberately limited and, like Jane Austen before him, if he refers to the great events taking place in the world around him, his interest is only in the extent to which they affect the lives of the small segment of society that falls beneath his observation.

Such a novel is not to everyone's taste, and it is probable that *The Wager* is the least read of the author's acknowledged masterpieces, perhaps largely due to the form in which he chose to present it. But it continues to exert its own fascination on

8

all true admirers of the master, who recognize the unique and delicate flavour which makes the connoisseur acclaim it vintage Machado.

R.L. Scott-Buccleuch
São Vicente
June, 1989

Preface

Those who have read my *Esau and Jacob* may perhaps remember these words from the preface: 'His spare moments he devoted to writing up his *Journal*, which despite some dull, tedious passages might serve (and perhaps does) to while away the time on the Petropolis ferry.'

I was referring to Counsellor Aires. Now that the *Journal* is about to be printed, it was felt that the section dealing with the two years, 1888–9, if pared of certain references, anecdotes, descriptions and reflections, might form a connected narrative that, despite its diary form, would be of interest. No time was wasted in editing it, as with the previous one, nor was much skill called for. It is presented exactly as written, apart from selection and abridgement, retaining only what is related to the main theme. The rest will appear one day, if there comes another day.

M. de A.

11

1888

Fancy that, it's exactly a year to the day since my return from Europe. What put me in mind of the date was hearing the cry of the street vendor selling brushes and dusters while I was having coffee: 'Brushes-o! Dusters-o!' I hear it most mornings, but on this occasion it reminded me of the day I disembarked here on my retirement, when I returned for good to my own country, to Catete and my own native tongue. It was the same cry I heard a year ago in 1887, possibly even from the same mouth.

During my thirty-odd years in the diplomatic service I sometimes came to Brazil on leave, but most of my time was spent in different countries overseas. I imagined I would end up being unable to accustom myself to life here again. But I did. To be sure, I often think of distant friends and places, customs and pastimes, but I can't say I miss them. Here is where I am; here I live, and here I shall die.

5 p.m.

I've just received a note from my sister Rita, which I will append to this:

9 January

My dear brother,
    I've only now remembered that it is a year today since you arrived home on retirement from Europe. It is too late now

13

to go to the family vault in São João Batista cemetery to give thanks for your safe return, so I'll go tomorrow morning in the hope that you will accompany me.

Your loving sister,
Rita

I see no need for this but I said I would go.

10 January

We went to the cemetery. Despite the cheerful nature of the occasion Rita could not help shedding some tears in memory of her husband, who lies there in the vault with my father and mother. She still loves him as much as on the day she lost him, all those years ago now. She had a lock of her hair buried in the coffin with him; it was black then: what was left out here has all turned white.

You couldn't call our vault ugly; it might be a little less ornate – just an inscription and a cross – but what there is is well done. If anything I found it too smart. Rita has it cleaned every month, which prevents it from ageing. Now in my opinion an old tomb gives a better idea of its function if it bears the marks of time, which is all-consuming. Otherwise it seems a creation of the day before.

Rita knelt and prayed there for some minutes while I gazed round at the nearby memorials. Nearly all bore the same appeal as did ours: 'Say a prayer for him'. . . . 'Say a prayer for her'. Later, on the way out, Rita told me that she usually complies with such requests, saying a prayer for all those strangers buried there. Quite likely it's the only one they get. She's a good-hearted soul, my sister, and a cheerful one too.

The impression given me by the cemetery as a whole was, like all others, that of complete immobility. The statues of angels and other figures were arrayed in varied attitudes, but all alike were motionless. The only signs of life were one or two birds chasing each other and fluttering in the branches, chirruping or singing. The bushes were silent, green and scattered with blossom.

Near the gate on the way out I told Rita of a woman I had

seen beside another tomb to the left of the main cross while she was praying. She was young, dressed in black and seemed to be praying too, with her hands folded in front of her. Her face was familiar but I couldn't place it. 'She's pretty and extremely elegant,' I said, with an enthusiasm learned in Rome.

'Where is she?'

When I told her, she wanted to find out who she was. Besides being good-hearted Rita is curious, though not so much so as to merit an Italian superlative. I suggested that we wait where we were at the gate.

'No, she may delay. Let's take a look at her from a distance. Is she really pretty?'

'She seemed to be.'

We walked back, threading our way between the tombstones. When we were a short way off, Rita came to a halt.

'Of course you know her. You met her at home just a few days ago.'

'Who is she?'

'Noronha's widow. Let's go before she sees us.'

Only then did I remember a woman Rita had introduced me to at Andaraí, and with whom I had conversed for a few minutes.

'He was a doctor, wasn't he?'

'That's right. She's the daughter of Baron Santa-Pia, a land-owner from Paraiba do Sul.'

Just then the widow moved her hands and seemed about to depart, but first she glanced about her as if to see whether she was alone. Perhaps she wanted to kiss her husband's name engraved on the tombstone, but there were people nearby, not counting two gravediggers carrying a watering can and a spade, who were discussing a funeral that same morning. Their raucous voices were audible as one said contemptuously: 'What, you carry one of those up the hill? You and three more like you, maybe.' Obviously they were referring to some heavy coffin, but I returned my attention to the widow, who was now walking away slowly without glancing back. From behind a monument I had no better view of her than I did at first. She made her way out through the gate, boarded a passing tram and was lost to sight. We followed close behind and caught the next tram.

It was then that Rita told me something of the girl's life and how happy she had been with her husband, now buried there for over two years. Their married life had been a short one. I don't know what perverse inspiration it was that prompted me to remark, 'That doesn't mean she won't marry again.'

'Not her. She won't marry again.'

'Who said so?'

'She won't marry again. You just have to remember their happy marriage, the life they led and all she suffered when he died.'

'That doesn't mean a thing; she can marry again. Widows can always marry again.'

'But I didn't.'

'You're different. There's only one you.'

Rita smiled, gazing at me reprovingly and shaking her head as she would at a mischievous child. Then her face clouded, for the remembrance of her husband always made her sad. I made a wager of it, and she, entering light-heartedly into the spirit of the thing, dared me to woo Noronha's widow myself. She bet she wouldn't have me.

'Don't forget I'm sixty-two years old.'

'You don't look it. No one would give you more than thirty or so.'

Soon after that we arrived home and Rita stayed to lunch. But before going to the table we returned to the subject of the widow's marriage, and she repeated her bet. With Goethe in mind I said to her, 'Rita dear, you are making the same wager with me as God did with Mephistopheles. Do you know it?'

'No.'

I went to my bookcase, took down the volume of Faust, opened the page at the prologue in heaven and read it to her, summarizing as best I could. Rita listened attentively to the wager of God and the Devil concerning Faust, the servant of the Lord, and of the inevitable fall the Crafty One had prepared for him. Rita is not well read, but she has a lively wit. What she had at that moment was a lively appetite. She laughed and said, 'Let's have lunch. I don't want to hear any more about your silly prologues. I stick to what I've already said, and you'll see for yourself whether what's been undone can ever be mended. Let's have lunch.'

We went in to lunch, and at two o'clock Rita returned to Andaraí. I wrote up these notes then took a stroll in town.

12 January

In relating my conversation with Rita yesterday I forgot to mention the part concerning my wife, who is buried over there in Vienna. For the second time Rita tried to persuade me to have her body brought to our vault, and once again I argued that although I should like to be near her, in my opinion the dead are best left wherever it is they happen to die. She retorted that they are better off among their own folk.

'When I die I shall go wherever she is, in the next world, and she will meet me there,' I said.

Rita smiled and cited the case of Noronha's widow, who had her husband's body brought from Lisbon, where he died, to Rio de Janeiro, where she herself expected to end her days. She said no more about the matter, but no doubt she will return to it until she gets her way. My brother-in-law used to say those were her tactics whenever she wanted anything.

Another thing I forgot was what she said about the Aguiars, a couple whose acquaintance I made during my last leave in Rio de Janeiro, and whom I had now met again. They are friends of both Rita and the widow, and in a couple of weeks or so from now will be celebrating their silver wedding. I have already visited them twice, visits which were returned by the husband. Rita spoke warmly of them and suggested I pay a formal visit on the occasion of their anniversary celebrations.

'You'll meet Fidelia there.'

'Who's Fidelia?'

'Noronha's widow.'

'Is that her name, Fidelia?'

'Yes.'

'Her name won't stop her from marrying again.'

'All the better for you since you will overcome her resistance and her name and end up marrying the lady. But I repeat what I said: she won't marry again.'

The only noteworthy thing in Fidelia's past is that her father and father-in-law were political enemies, being heads of rival parties in Paraiba do Sul. Animosity between families has never prevented young people from falling in love, witness Verona and other places. And even of Verona it is said that the families of Romeo and Juliet were formerly friends and of the same party. They also say that they never existed except in tales or in Shakespeare's imagination.

In our Brazilian towns, throughout the length and breadth of the country, I don't know of a single case. The hostility of the parents is handed down to the offspring, who preserve the unity of the family by seeking no outside attachments, and will poison their enemy's terrain if they can. If I were capable of hatred, that is how I should hate. But I hate nothing and no one: 'perdono a tutti', as they say in the opera.

Now, how it was that they came to fall in love – these two from Paraiba do Sul – Rita never told me, and it would be interesting to find out. Law and farming providing us with a Romeo and Juliet here in Rio – our Romeo's father was a lawyer in the town of Paraiba – is one of those situations which need a full description to be understood to our satisfaction. And as Rita never volunteered these details I shall have to ask her for them. She may well refuse, imagining I am already sighing my heart out for the lady.

As I was rushing out of the Do Sul Bank I met Aguiar, the manager, on his way in. He greeted me warmly, asked after Rita and we chatted for several minutes.

That was yesterday. This morning I received an invitation from him and his wife to dine with them on the 24th. It is their silver wedding. 'Just an informal dinner for a few friends', he wrote. I learned later that it is to be a small, intimate party. Rita is going too, so I decided to accept. Yes, I'll go.

Three days confined to the house on account of a cold and a touch of fever. I'm better today and according to the doctor will be able to go out tomorrow. But as for the Aguiars' silver wedding party, the ever-cautious Dr Silva advised me against going. Rita, who looked after me for two days, is of the same opinion. But since she was not too opposed to the idea, if I find myself stronger and well enough, as is quite possible, it will take a lot to keep me away. We'll see: three days pass quickly.

6 p.m.

I spent the day browsing through books, in particular re-reading some pages of Shelley, also of Thackeray. The one consoled me for the other, while the latter served as a corrective to the former. In this way one mind complements another, and the spirit learns the language of the spirit.

9 p.m.

Rita dined with me, and I told her that I felt as sound as a bell and quite strong enough to go to the Aguiars' party. After recommending that I took care, she agreed that I might go provided I had no turn for the worse and ate discreetly at dinner. In any case my eyes would be on a meagre diet.

'I don't think Fidelia is going,' she explained.

'Not going?'

'I was with Judge Campos today and he told me his niece had her customary attack of neuralgia. She suffers from neuralgia. When she gets it it lasts for days, and it takes a lot of medicine and patience to get rid of it. I'll maybe call on her tomorrow or the day after.'

Rita added that her absence would be a sad blow to the Aguiars, who were counting on her to be one of the attractions of the party. They are very fond of her, as she is of them, and they seem to be well suited. That is Rita's opinion and likely to be mine too, as I told her.

'If I feel free to do so I'll make a habit of visiting them. They're a nice couple, the Aguiars. Didn't they ever have any children?'

'No. And they are so affectionate, Dona Carmo even more so than her husband. You can't imagine how close they are. I don't go there more often because I tend to keep to myself, but the few visits I pay are enough to show what a wonderful couple they are, she in particular. Judge Campos, who has known them for a great many years, can vouch for them.'

'Will there be many people at the dinner?'

'No, just a few I think. Most of the guests will be going at night. They are unpretentious: the dinner is just for their closest friends, so their inviting you shows a very sincere regard.'

I felt that when I was introduced to them seven years ago, but at that time I thought it was more in respect of the Minister than the man. Now, when they greeted me it was with real pleasure. Well, I shall go there on the 24th, Fidelia or no Fidelia.

25 January

Yesterday I went to the party. Let's see if I can summarize my impressions of the evening.

These could not be better, beginning with the harmony between the old couple. I know it's a risky business to judge the relationship of two people on the strength of a few hours spent at a party. The occasion naturally brings back memories of old times, and the affection of others serves to increase their own. But that was not the case. Theirs was something of a higher order and different from the joy around them. I felt that the passage of the years had strengthened and refined nature so that these two people were in fact one, a single being. I did not feel this, nor could I, on entering the house – it was impressed on me during the evening.

Aguiar came to greet me at the door, it seemed with the intention of embracing me, had this been permissible in such a place; but it was his hand performed this function, for he shook mine effusively. He is already turned sixty (she is fifty), stocky rather than thin, lively, courteous and of cheerful disposition. He took me to meet his wife, who was talking with two friends at one side of the room. The old lady's charm was already known to me, but this time the nature of the occasion and the tone of my greeting brought to her face an expression which fully justified the use of the term radiant. With a quick glance at her husband she gave me her hand, inclining her head as she listened to me.

I felt myself the object of the attentions of both. Rita arrived shortly after I did, as well as other guests, all known to me, and who I saw were friends of the house. In the middle of the conversation I overheard an unexpected comment from one lady to another: 'I do hope Fidelia hasn't taken a turn for the worse.'

'Is she coming?' asked the other.

'She said she would. She's better, but it might be unwise for her to come.'

The remainder of what they had to say concerning the widow was more encouraging. I barely heard what one of the guests was saying to me, noting merely the subject and giving the appearance of attention. As it was almost time for dinner I concluded that Fidelia was not coming. I was wrong. Fidelia and her uncle were the last to arrive, but there they were. The fuss Dona Carmo made over her showed clearly how happy she was to see her there, barely convalescent and with the danger of returning after nightfall. The old couple were obviously delighted.

Fidelia was not entirely out of mourning. She wore coral earrings, and the brooch on her breast with the portrait of her husband was of gold. The rest of her dress and ornaments were subdued. The jewels and posy of myosotis at her waist she probably wore as a compliment to her friend. That morning she had sent a note of congratulations together with a small porcelain vase, which now stood on a dresser with the other anniversary presents.

Seeing her now I found her no less intriguing than in the cemetery or in Rita's house, and no less attractive either. Her body seems finely sculptured, not in the sense of rigidity; just the opposite, for it has suppleness. I refer merely to the perfection of her figure (those lines which are visible – the remainder can be confidently guessed at). Her complexion is soft and pale, with a colouring in the cheeks very becoming in a widow. That is what I noted on her arrival, together with her black eyes and hair; the rest came as the evening advanced, until she took her leave. Nothing more was needed to complete the picture of a creature as interesting in appearance as she was in conversation. That, at any rate, is the conclusion I reached after several moments' examination. Actually I was not thinking in prose but in verse, and in fact a verse of Shelley's that I had re-read some days earlier at home as I mentioned before; it was taken from one of his stanzas of 1821:

I can give not what men call love.

I murmured it to myself in the original, then repeated the poet's confession in prose, adding an envoi of my own composition: 'I cannot give what men call love . . . the more's the pity.'

This confession made me not a whit less cheerful, so when Dona Carmo took my arm I accompanied her as if it were to a wedding dinner. Aguiar gave his arm to Fidelia, and sat between her and his wife. I note these details with no other purpose but to point out that husband and wife sat together with Fidelia on one side and myself on the other. In this manner we heard the twin beat of their hearts – a hyperbole I permit myself to emphasize that we both, or I at least, shared the happiness of those twenty-five years of peace and consolation.

Our hostess, gentle, sweet-natured and amiable towards everyone, seemed genuinely happy on her anniversary, as did her husband. He may have been even happier than she but was without the means to express it. Dona Carmo has the gift of self-expression in her whole being, allied to a power of attraction that I have met in very few women. Her white hair, arranged neatly and tastefully, gave to old age a particular distinction, uniting as it were all ages in one. I don't think I am expressing myself very well, but it is hardly necessary to clarify matters for the sake of the flames to which the notes of a lonely old man will eventually be consigned.

From time to time she and her husband exchanged glances, and occasionally the odd word. Only once did these looks carry an expression of sadness, and later Rita gave me the explanation. One of the guests – there is always one who is indiscreet – on proposing a toast, alluded to their lack of children, saying, 'God denied them these that they should love each other the more.' He didn't speak in verse, though the idea might well have been

22

set to rhyme, an art he possibly cultivated in his youth. He was about fifty and the father of a son. On hearing his words the old couple looked sadly at each other, but soon rallied and were smiling and laughing again. Rita later told me that that was their only cause for regret. I think Fidelia too noticed their sad faces, for I saw her turn towards Dona Carmo and raise her glass in a charming gesture.

'Your health,' she said.

The old lady was so touched she could only reply with a gesture, and it was moments after she had raised her own glass to her lips that she was able to answer in a choked voice, a single word: 'Thank you.'

All this was done in an aside, almost in secret. Aguiar accepted his share of the toast in good part, and the dinner ended with no further cause for melancholy.

At night more guests arrived, and three or four sat down to cards. I stayed in the living room observing that gathering of cheerful men and elderly and youthful women, distinguished among whom were Dona Carmo for the serenity of her old age, and Fidelia for the graceful charm of her youth. Fidelia's charm, however, still bore the imprint of widowhood, now of two years' standing. Shelley continued to murmur in my ear, and I repeated to myself: 'I can give not what men call love.'

When I mentioned this to Rita she declared it to be the usual excuse of the bad debtor, in other words, realizing myself unable to overcome the girl's resistance I made out that I was incapable of loving. With this she began another panegyric on Fidelia's conjugal felicity: 'Everyone who ever knew them can tell you what a happy couple they were,' she went on. 'And when you think that they married against the wishes of their families, both of which treated them spitefully! Dona Carmo has been a close friend of Fidelia, and though she is too discreet to repeat her confidences the little she feels able to tell is evidence of her admiration and respect. I've heard her many a time on the subject. Fidelia even talks to me about it occasionally. Have a word with her uncle. . . . He'll be able to tell you something about the Aguiars too . . .'

At this point I interrupted her: 'From what I'm told, while I was travelling around representing Brazil overseas the country was becoming a veritable Abraham's bosom. You, the Aguiars, the Noronhas, in short every married couple, were turning yourselves into models of eternal bliss.'

'Well go and ask the Judge; he'll tell you all about it.'

'Another impression I have formed in this house tonight is that the two ladies, the married one and the widow, love each other like mother and daughter, isn't that so?'

'Yes, I think so.'

'Does the widow also have no children?'

'No, she hasn't. That's another thing they have in common.'

'There's a point of dissimilarity with Fidelia being a widow.'

'Oh no. Fidelia's widowhood is just like Dona Carmo's old age. But if you consider it a dissimilarity it's in your hands to put matters right by rescuing her from her widowhood if you can. But I repeat, you won't be able to.'

My sister is not given to witticisms, but when she comes out with one it is usually barbed. That's what I said to her then as I saw her into the coach that would take her to Andaraí, while I walked home to Catete. I forgot to mention that the Aguiars' house is on Flamengo beach. It's old but solidly built and stands in a small garden.

Saturday

Yesterday I met an old friend from the diplomatic corps and promised to dine with him tomorrow in Petropolis. I'll go up today and come back on Monday. Unfortunately I woke up feeling out of sorts and would much prefer to stay rather than travel. But maybe the change of air and scenery will do me good. Life is a tiring business, especially when you're old.

Monday

Today I came back from Petropolis. On Saturday as the ferryboat left Prainha I met Judge Campos on board, which was lucky for me as before long my ill humour had vanished and I arrived at Mauá well on the road to recovery. By the time I reached Petropolis station I was back to my normal self.

24

I don't know whether I have already mentioned in this journal that Campos was my class-mate at school in São Paulo. With time and going our different ways we lost contact, so that when we met again last year, apart from our school-day recollections, we were strangers. Nowadays we see each other occasionally and spend an evening together in Flamengo, but our different lives have completed the work of time and separation.

On the ferryboat we managed to straighten the old ties. A journey by land and sea gave ample opportunity to recall our school-days. Sufficient to enable us to forget our old age for a while.

As we climbed into the mountains our impressions differed somewhat. Campos delighted in the train journey. I confessed that I liked it better when we made the trip in carriages drawn by mules, one behind the other, not for the sake of the vehicle itself, but because of the glorious views of the sea and the city that were gradually unfolded far below. The train carries you up in one frantic rush right to Petropolis station. And I remembered the halts *en route*, here to have a coffee, there to drink water at the celebrated spring, and finally the scene at the top, where the smart society of Petropolis were waiting to accompany us in their carriages or on horseback into the city. Some of the passengers from the capital used to transfer there and then into the carriages of the families who were waiting for them.

Campos carried on praising the pleasures and advantages of the railway: 'Just think of the time we save!' I was tempted to reply by pointing out the time that we waste, but it would have started a dispute that would have made the journey even shorter and duller. I preferred to change the subject and, savouring the last few minutes, spoke about progress. He did too, so that we both arrived highly pleased with ourselves in the highland city.

We stayed at the same hotel (the Bragança). After dinner we went for a stroll beside the river to digest our meal. Then, referring to the old days, I mentioned the Aguiars and that Rita had told me he knew them well when they were both young. I said I considered them a perfect example of a happily married couple. My secret intention was perhaps to pass from them to the details and circumstances of his own niece's marriage, a difficult subject to broach without displaying undue curiosity, which is not my normal custom. But he gave me neither time nor opportunity for he could talk of nothing but the Aguiars. I listened patiently because after his first few words I began to take an interest, and the Judge himself is an agreeable speaker. But it is too late to record what he said. I'll leave it for another day when the first impression has passed and my memory will have retained only the essentials.

4 February

Today I must summarize what the Judge told me in Petropolis about the Aguiars. I shan't include isolated incidents or anecdotes, and I shall even omit the adjectives, which sounded better in his mouth than if recorded by my pen. What I shall write is only what is needful to understand the persons and facts involved.

I say this because I am concerned with the personal life of the old couple, linked as it is with that of the widow, Fidelia. Their biographical details are briefly as follows. Aguiar was a book-keeper when he married. Dona Carmo lived with her mother, who was from Nova Friburgo, and her father, a Swiss watchmaker in the same city. Everyone approved the match. Aguiar remained a book-keeper, passing from one firm to another, was made a partner in the last one, finally became a bank manager, and they reached their old age without having any children. That's all there is to it, nothing more. They have lived to this day without discord or misunderstandings.

They were fond of each other, and have always been so despite their mutual jealousies, or perhaps because of them. From the time she was a young girl in love, Dona Carmo exercised an influence over Aguiar that all such girls do in this world, and perhaps in the next too if by chance they exist there. Aguiar once told the Judge of the hard times when, with their engagement confirmed, he lost his job as a result of his employer going bankrupt. He had to look for another, and though this did not take long his new job did not permit him to marry right away as he needed time to settle down and gain confidence. His character was like individual blocks of stone, hers the lime and cement which held them together in those critical days. This image is taken from Campos, who said he had it from Aguiar himself. Lime and cement were to be invaluable to him every time the stones got separated. He knew his own mind, but in difficult times she was always there to offer comfort and advice.

The first years of their married life were not easy. Aguiar took up various part-time jobs to help eke out his inadequate earnings. Dona Carmo took charge of the house, assisting the servants and arranging matters so as to secure those comforts there was no money to provide. Economical and practical, she organized the household so methodically and so thoroughly as to win the admiration of her husband and her guests. Gracefully combining the decorative with the utilitarian, each item faithfully and accurately reflected her own personality. Table cloths and carpets, curtains and suchlike which came in later years, all bore the hallmark of her workmanship and the impress of her personality. Had it been necessary, she might be said to have invented what could be called elegant poverty.

They built up a varied circle of friends, kindly, unpretentious folk like themselves. In this Dona Carmo played a bigger part than Aguiar. She had been the same as a child. At the college in Engenho Novo, where she studied, she was declared to be its most outstanding pupil, and this without arousing the envy, secret or avowed, of a single one of her school-mates, but with the open approbation of all the present and former pupils. It was as if all of them identified with her. Was she then some intellectual prodigy? Not at all: in intelligence she was above the average, but not to the extent of dwarfing her companions. Everything was the result of her warm, affectionate disposition.

It was this which made her so attractive and companionable. One thing which Campos told me I had already noted for myself during the anniversary party, which was that Dona Carmo won the hearts of women both young and old. There are old women who do not know how to get along with the young, and girls who will have nothing to do with their elders. Aguiar's wife is equally at home with all; that's how she was as a young girl, and that's how she is in her old age.

Campos was not always with them, even in the early days, but after he became a regular guest at the house he was able to observe the maturing of the bride and newly-wedded wife, and to understand her husband's adoration of her. Aguiar was a happy man, finding in her conversation a relief from the worries and stress of the world, and seeking no sweeter inspiration than a glance from her eyes. She had that happy knack of restoring him to peace and normality.

One day at their house, on opening a collection of Italian poems, Campos found an old scrap of paper with some verses written on it. Somewhat abashed, they told him that these had been copied from the book by Dona Carmo before their wedding. He replaced the paper in the book and returned the book to the shelf. They were both fond of poetry, and perhaps she wrote some which got thrown away together with her last youthful indiscretions. They seemed to have an instinctive talent for poetry, but lacked the means for adequate expression.

That last observation is mine, not Judge Campos's, and is made merely to conclude this portrait of the couple. Not that poetry is a necessary adjunct to manners, but it can add charm. My next question to the Judge was whether they had any regrets. He replied that they had one, just one, but it was all-important: they had no children.

'Rita said the same thing.'

'They never had any children,' repeated Campos.

They both wanted a child, she more than him, even if it were just one. Dona Carmo's affection was all-embracing – the conjugal, the filial and the maternal. Campos had even met her mother, whose portrait, framed together with her father's, hung in the living room. Dona Carmo spoke of them tenderly, with long, heavy sighs. She had no brothers or sisters, but fraternal affection was what she extended to all her friends. As for children, or the lack of them, the truth is there was much of the mother in the affection she bestowed as a wife and friend. It is no less true that for this inverted orphanhood she now has a consolation.

'Dona Fidelia?'

'Yes, Fidelia. And there used to be another, but that's all over now.'

This led to a further story, which could be told in half a dozen lines: not so few with evening drawing in, but I'll set it down quickly.

When Dona Carmo was twenty or so, one of her friends gave birth to a son. For reasons which Campos did not see fit to dwell on the mother and son spent some time in the Aguiars' house. By the end of the first week the child had two mothers, and since the real one had to join her husband in Minas – a few days' journey away – Dona Carmo persuaded her friend to leave the child and its nurse with her. These were the first bonds of affection, which would later grow with time and habit. The father was a dealer in coffee, and at that time was on business trip in Minas. The mother was a native of Taubaté, São Paulo, who loved travelling on horseback. When the time came to christen the baby, Luisa Guimarães invited her friend to be godmother. This was exactly what Dona Carmo wanted; she accepted joyfully, her husband with pleasure, and the christening took place as if it were a celebration of the Aguiar family.

Tristão – that was the name of her godson – spent his childhood divided between two mothers and two houses. Years passed, and Dona Carmo's hopes of a family faded. Tristão was the son which fortune had declined to bless them with, said Aguiar one day. His wife, catholic even in her language, amended this to Providence, and doted even more on her godson. According to Campos, in the opinion of some people, and I agree with them, Dona Carmo seemed more of a mother than the mother herself. The boy divided his attentions between the two, with perhaps a slight preference for his godmother. The reason was no doubt that there he was more thoroughly spoiled, had all his wishes gratified and was well supplied with sweets – all excellent motives for the child as well as the adult. When the time came for him to go to school, since the Aguiars' house was nearer he would go there for his dinner before returning to Laranjeiras, where the Guimarães lived. Sometimes his godmother accompanied him.

During the child's two or three illnesses Dona Carmo suffered extreme distress. I use the same adjective Campos employed, though I consider it exaggerated and I hate exaggeration. One thing that I must say of Dona Carmo is that she is one of those few people of whom it is never said that they are 'mad about strawberries', or 'dying to hear Mozart'. With her the intensity was in the emotion felt, not in its expression. Be that as it may, Campos was present during the boy's last childhood illness, which happened to be in his godmother's house, and saw for himself all Dona Carmo's distress, her tenderness and her fears, some moments of anguish and tears, and finally the joy of recovery. But his mother was still his mother, and no doubt suffered too, though according to Campos not so much. There is an affection which is not so demonstrative, more under control, which does not reveal itself to everyone.

Sickness, joys, hopes, all the varied experiences of Tristão's early years affected the two godparents, but especially the godmother, as if he had been of their own flesh and blood. It was their son, who was now ten years old, now eleven, now twelve, growing in size and understanding. When he was thirteen, on learning that his father intended putting him into business, he ran to his godmother declaring that he didn't want a career in business.

'Why not, my child?'

Dona Carmo used this mode of address, which her age and spiritual relationship permitted, without usurping anyone else's rights. Tristão answered that his ambition was elsewhere. He wanted to be a lawyer. His godmother argued his father's case, but with her Tristão was wont to be more outspoken than with his father or mother, and insisted that he wanted to study law and be a lawyer. Even if he had no proper vocation for the law the idea of it attracted him.

'I want to be a lawyer! I want to be a lawyer!'

Dona Carmo ended up agreeing with him and took up her godson's cause. His father was not to be convinced. 'Isn't business an honourable profession, and a lucrative one too? Besides, he won't be starting from scratch like others have had to, including his own father – he'll have me to support him.'

He produced other arguments, which Dona Carmo listened to without contesting, she insisted simply that the important thing was to have the inclination, and if the boy didn't have that the best thing was to give way and let him do what he had a taste for. After a few days Tristão's father gave way, Dona Carmo wanting to be the first to give the boy the good news. The happiness was all hers.

Five or six months later Tristão's father decided to put forward a journey he had planned for the following year to visit his family in Lisbon; his mother had fallen ill. Tristão, who was preparing to begin his studies, no sooner learned of the forthcoming trip than he insisted on accompanying them. It was his yearning for novelty, his curiosity to see Europe, something different from the streets of Rio de Janeiro, so familiar and so boring. Mother and father alike refused, but the boy insisted. He again had resort to Dona Carmo, but this time, fearful of being separated from him albeit temporarily, she sided with his parents and counselled that he remain. Even Aguiar was drawn into the dispute, but there was no arguing with the lad. Tristão was determined at all costs to embark for Lisbon.

'Father will be coming back in six months' time and I'll come with him. What are six months?'

'What about your studies?' said Aguiar. 'You'll lose a whole year. . . .'

'Alright, I'll lose a year. A year is no great sacrifice compared with the thrill of a trip to Europe.'

At this Dona Carmo had an inspiration. She promised that as soon as he graduated she would take him on a trip not of just six months but of a year or more. He would have time to see everything, the new and the old, different countries, seas, customs. . . . But he must study first. Tristão was not to be persuaded. He had his way despite the tears that it cost.

I will not enter into details concerning these parting tears, nor the promises made, the keepsakes given, the portraits exchanged between the boy and his godparents. All this was done on both sides, but not all the promises were kept. If letters arrived with news and greetings, the boy himself did not. His parents extended their stay longer than originally planned, and Tristão entered the School of Medicine in Lisbon. He was to be neither a businessman nor a lawyer.

Aguiar concealed the news from his wife as long as he could in the hope that he might devise some scheme to change the course of destiny and bring the lad back to Brazil. But there was nothing to be done and he himself could no longer conceal his grief. When he communicated the bitter news to his wife without being able to add any word of hope or comfort she wept inconsolably. Tristão wrote to tell them of his change of profession, promising to return to Brazil once he had graduated. But from then on his letters became few and far between until they ceased altogether. No letters, no memories, and probably no regrets either. Guimarães returned alone in order to wind up his affairs, and then embarked again never more to return.

5 February

On re-reading what I wrote yesterday I find I could have been more concise, in particular omitting all those tears. I don't like tears, and can't remember ever shedding any, unless it was for my mother when I was a child. They were real enough, so I'll leave those that I have already noted, as well as the portrait of Tristão, to which I promised half a dozen lines and ended up devoting the greater part. There's nothing worse than idle folk – or retired ones, which is the same thing. Time lies heavy upon them, and once they put their hand to writing no amount of paper will serve their turn.

However, I haven't mentioned everything. It occurs to me that I omitted one thing in Campos's story. I didn't speak of Aguiar's shares in the Do Sul Bank, nor his other stock, the houses he owns and his earnings as manager – an estate worth two hundred or so contos. That's what Campos told me on the river bank in Petropolis. He's an interesting man is Campos: if his talents are few it is no matter since he knows how to make the most of those he has. Admittedly by this rule we should have to accept a whole range of insipid characters, but Campos is not one of those.

There's one other thing I forgot to write on the 4th, but which was not included in Campos's story. It was when I was saying goodbye to him, for he was staying on in Petropolis for three or four more days. When I asked him to convey my best wishes to his niece, he said, 'She's with the Aguiars. She spent yesterday afternoon and last night with them and plans to stay until my return.'

What different attitudes! The Aguiars longed for children while I never gave them a second thought, and though I am alone in the world do not feel their lack. Then there are those who wanted them, had them, and didn't know how to keep them.

Yesterday I went to Andaraí for dinner, and recounted my conversation with the Judge to Rita.

'Didn't he mention his niece?'

'He had barely enough time to tell me about the Aguiars.'

'Well, I found out what I wanted to know about Fidelia. It was Dona Carmo herself who told me.'

'If this story is going to be as long as hers . . .'

'It isn't; it's much shorter. I can tell it in five minutes.'

I took out my watch to see the exact time and check the duration of her narrative. Rita began, and ten minutes later had finished. Exactly double the time. But the subject – Fidelia's marriage – was a fascinating one, and the widow interested me.

'They met here in Rio,' said Rita, 'never having seen each other in the country. Fidelia was staying with the Judge (her aunt was still living then), and the young fellow, Eduardo, was studying at the School of Medicine. The first time he saw her was from the gallery of the Lyric Theatre, where he had gone with a group of students. She was sitting with her aunt in the front row of a box. He saw her again, she noticed him and they ended up falling in love. When they each found out who the other was, the harm was already done, but probably it would have been just the same had they known from the start because it was a case of love at first sight. When Fidelia's father came to Rio he learned of the affair from his brother, who cautiously told him what he suspected, at the same time hinting that it was a good opportunity for reconciliation between the two families. The Baron was furious and marched the girl straight back to the fazenda. You can't imagine what happened then.'

'I can. I can.'

'Oh no you can't.'

'He strapped her to the whipping post?'

'Of course not,' said Rita. 'He didn't go beyond threatening her with words, but harsh words, warning her that he would put her out of the house unless she gave up such a preposterous notion. Fidelia declared repeatedly that she was engaged to be married and would wed Eduardo come what may. Her mother opposed her too and sided with her father. Refusing to give in, Fidelia protested no further but spent days shut up in her room, weeping. The female slaves, seeing her tears, suspected a love affair and even guessed the name of the young man, though this they may have overheard from their masters. Finally the girl refused to eat, whereupon her mother, fearing for her health, took up her cause with her husband. But the father declared he would rather see her dead or out of her mind than consent to the mingling of his blood with that of the Noronhas. For their part the Noronhas were no less opposed to the match. When he learned of his son's passion for the Baron's daughter Eduardo's father informed him that he would put him out on the street if he persisted in such an outrageous idea.'

'As enemies they were well worthy of each other,' I commented.

'They were that,' said Rita. 'When the Judge heard what was going on he went to the fazenda and, having confirmed the truth, told his brother that it was pointless to oppose the match because once his daughter was of age she would be able to leave home anyway. No one was asking him to humiliate himself before the Noronhas or make peace with them, just to allow the young people to marry and go wherever they wanted. But the Baron dug his heels in, and the Judge was about to return to Rio without completing the mission he had undertaken to accomplish when Fidelia fell sick. Her illness was serious, and the cure made difficult by her refusal to take either food or medicine. . . . But what are you smiling at? Don't you believe me?'

'Oh I do, I assure you. I find it romantic. In any case I am interested in the girl. You were saying, the cure was difficult?'

'Yes. Her mother decided to beg her father to give way, and he finally did so on the understanding that he would never receive her or speak to her again; he would not go to the wedding and wanted nothing more to do with her. On her recovery Fidelia went with her uncle and was married the following year. The bridegroom's father also declared that he never wanted to see them again.'

'So much strife for such a short spell of happiness.'

'That's true. Their happiness was great but it was short-lived. One day they decided to go to Europe, and that's when it was that Eduardo died unexpectedly in Lisbon, and Fidelia had his body brought back here. You saw her there beside his grave; she often goes there. Even then her father, who was a widower himself by that time, refused to see her. Fidelia tried first on her own, then later with her uncle, but it was no use. He never saw her or spoke to her again. The only thing I wasn't sure of was what happened on the fazenda, but that's the story. Now tell me if she's the kind of widow who will marry again?'

'Not with any Tom, Dick or Harry, no. At least, I doubt it. But a personable young man . . .' I said, preening myself and laughing.

'Are you still thinking . . .'

'Who, me? What I'm thinking of is your dinner, which I'm sure will be delicious. What impresses me about your story is that this girl is not only pretty, she's stubborn. But for me your soup is worth more than all the aesthetic and moral considerations in this world or the next.'

Over dinner I told Rita what the Judge had said about his niece spending several days in Flamengo, and asked whether she was really so intimate with the Aguiars.

'Oh yes, no doubt about it. Once Fidelia fell ill in Flamengo and stayed there to convalesce. Having given up all hope of their godson, Tristão, who had completely forgotten about them, they became more and more attached to Fidelia. Dona Carmo simply dotes on her. You remember the anniversary party, don't you? Aguiar doesn't call her "daughter" so as not to seem to usurp that title from her real father, but since she has no mother his wife has no such qualms. And Fidelia seems to want no other mother.'

11 February

In the old days, when I was a child, I heard it said that children were only given the names of saints. But Fidelia . . . ? I know of no saint of that name, or pagan woman either for that matter. Could the Baron's daughter have been given the feminine form of *Fidelio* in honour of Beethoven? It's possible, though I doubt him capable of such inspiration and artistic allusion. Neither can I find the family name, which appears in their title, Santa-Pia, in any list of canonized saints. The only person I know of that name is Dante: *Ricorditi de me, chi son la Pia.*

It appears that we no longer want our Anas or Marias, our Catarinas or Joanas, but are devising a new onomasticon to provide us with greater variety. Fashion rules everything in this world, except the stars and me, and I am the same old fellow I always was, except for the diplomatic work which I no longer have.

13 February

Campos told me today that his brother had written to him secretly saying that out there on the fazenda he'd heard a rumour about a forthcoming law abolishing slavery. Campos himself doesn't think this Ministry will do anything about it, and there is no prospect of another just yet.

14 February

Today's date (anniversary of the revolution of 1848) reminds me of the celebrations we lads held in São Paulo, and the toast I proposed to the great Lamartine. Ah, the days of our youth! When I mentioned this to the Judge, he said, 'My brother believes we are heading for a revolution here too, and with it the Republic.'

I've just come from the Aguiars' house. Fidelia was there, together with a cousin of hers, the Judge's son (sixteen years old), who is a student at the Naval College and an employee of the Bank of Brazil. I stayed there a good hour or more. The old lady was charming, as was the girl, and the conversation avoided any topic that might remind either of their respective losses, the one of her husband, the other of her godson. They told stories about their acquaintance, which I listened to with a smile or a look of concern as the occasion demanded. I too told one of distant parts, but in my anxiety not to remind the widow of places she might have visited with her husband I was obliged to curtail the story and not to embark on another. However, two or three times she spoke of her experiences abroad, impressions of what she had seen in museums in Italy and Germany. Of our own country we said the pleasantest things and were always in perfect agreement. Even the tower of Gloria Church, which some had defended as being necessary, caused the two of us to agree to disagree without me having to attack anyone at all. The Aguiars listened to us smiling, while the lad from the Naval College tried unsuccessfully to shift the conversation to military matters.

With this and other things we passed the evening. No one asked Fidelia to play, though I am told she is a gifted pianist. In compensation she spoke to us about musicians and well-known compositions, but briefly and hesitatingly, possibly because it reminded her of her late husband.

10 March

There's been a change of cabinet after all. Counsellor João Alfredo made up a new one today. In three or four days I'll go and pay my respects to the new Foreign Minister.

20 March

Judge Campos thinks something will be done about freeing the slaves – a step in that direction at least. Aguiar, who was with us, says he has heard nothing in town, nor has any news reached the Do Sul Bank.

Santa-Pia arrived from the fazenda but didn't go to his brother's house; he went to the America Hotel. Obviously he doesn't want to meet his daughter. Nothing dies so hard as a long-cherished hatred. It seems he came on account of a rumour going about in Paraiba do Sul concerning the emancipation of the slaves.

I heard that the Baron has fallen ill and his brother has managed to persuade him to go to his house. This is how it came about. He didn't invite him when he first arrived, but then found a means of letting him know that Fidelia was away, staying with a friend, and would not be returning for some time. When he suggested he remove to his house to convalesce he refused at first, then later accepted. All this had been previously arranged with Fidelia, so now she is installed in Flamengo with the Aguiars, thus leaving Campos's house free for her wrathful and ailing father. Campos and Aguiar are of the opinion that he'll end up being reconciled to his daughter, but at the moment they don't meet, much to her regret.

Now, I ask myself, was it worth the trouble of offending a father in exchange for a husband who had no sooner initiated her into the mysteries of love than he retired from the scene and died? Obviously not. And if I offered to conclude her course for her she and her father would be reconciled. Ah, but then it would be necessary not to have forgotten what I learned and then promptly forgot – everything, or almost everything. *I can give not . . .* (Shelley).

Absentmindedness can be the devil. It happened to me when I was coming from the city, and I only came to myself when the tram stopped in Largo do Machado. I jumped off, and before walking back the way we had come, I delayed for a moment to slip through the garden towards Gloria Church to have a look at its façade and tower. I did so remembering my conversation with Fidelia the other evening in Flamengo.

A little ahead of me two ladies seemed to be doing the same thing. They looked round and proved to be none other than Fidelia and Dona Carmo. They were not wearing hats, having just walked from the house. They saw me, and I walked up to them. We spoke little – news of the Baron, who is better, and Aguiar, who is well – then parted.

I walked towards Catete while they continued in the direction of the church. They were still not very distant when it occurred to me to glance back. Could I have done otherwise? This is where I would need to understand all that philosophers have told us about free will, so as to deny it once again, before succumbing at the point where it loses even the appearance of credibility. This page would have had quite a different ending. But it was not to be. I will say merely that, unable to control my head or eyes, I saw the two ladies, their arms round each other's waists, strolling leisurely and lovingly together.

8 April

Journal, my faithful journal, do not record all that this idle pen of mine indites. In wishing to serve me you will end up rendering me a disservice, for if it should happen that I depart this life with no time to consign you to the flames, those who read me before the Seventh Day Mass, or even before my burial, might suppose I am confiding a lover's sighs.

No, dear journal. Whenever you find that note creeping in, leap from my desk and fly. The open window will show you a stretch of roof between the street and the sky, and there or elsewhere you will find a resting place. As for me, the most to be hoped for is to be forgotten, which is something, but not all: before that will come the scoffs of mischief-makers and the merely idle.

Listen to me, my journal. What attracts me about that young lady, Fidelia, is mainly a certain air she has, something to do with that fleeting smile she displays occasionally. I want to observe her if I get the chance. I have all the time in the world, but you know that that is little enough for me, for my man José, for you with leisure time – it's all too little.

Astonishing news. The reason for the Baron's visit is to consult the Judge about the immediate liberation of all Santa-Pia's slaves. That's what I've just heard; and more, the principal motive for the consultation is merely the drawing up of the deed. As his brother doubted the wisdom of this, he asked the Baron what had driven him to it since he had always condemned the Government's supposed intention to decree abolition. The answer he received was as follows, and I don't know whether to consider it subtle, profound, both of these or neither.

'I do so to show that I consider it an act of confiscation, the Government's interfering with the legitimate rights of the owner, and I use these even to my own detriment, of my own free will, and because I have the power to do so.'

Could it be the certainty of abolition that forces Santa-Pia to act in this way, anticipating by several weeks or months the decree itself? To someone who put this question Campos replied no. 'No,' he said. 'My brother believes in the Government's intentions, but not in the consequences, other than chaos on the fazendas. His act simply expresses the sincerity of his convictions and his own violent temperament. He is capable of suggesting that all masters free their slaves immediately, and the next day of proposing the downfall of the Government for attempting to do so by law.'

Campos had an idea. He reminded his brother that by freeing his slaves now he would be prejudicing his daughter, who was his heir. Santa-Pia looked thoughtful. It was not his purpose to deny his daughter her eventual right to the slaves, but he probably found it annoying that in such a situation along should come Fidelia to complicate matters. After a few moments' hesitation he drew a deep breath and replied that until he was dead everything he owned was his and his alone. Seeing he was adamant, the Judge acceded to his request and together they drew up the deed of enfranchisement.

With the paper in his hand, Santa-Pia said, 'I'm sure that only a few will leave the fazenda. Most will stay on with me to earn the salary I'll offer them, and some even for nothing – just for the pleasure of dying where they were born.'

When Fidelia heard of her father's action she wanted to see him, not to condemn but to embrace him, so unconcerned was she for any future loss. Her uncle dissuaded her, saying that her father was still very angry with her.

Santa-Pia is not such an ill-favoured old man; in fact he's not all that old, being younger than me. He gasps for breath sometimes, but that may be due to bronchitis. He's stocky, broad-shouldered, with calloused hands and growing bald.

We recognized each other, I before he did, perhaps because Europe has changed me more. He remembered the time when, as his brother's school-mate, I dined with him here in Rio. His brother had already spoken about me, reminding him of our former acquaintance. He told me that in three days' time he would be returning to the fazenda, and offered his hospitality should I ever wish to honour him with a visit. I thanked him and gave my promise, though without committing myself, and with no intention of ever going there. It takes a good deal to drag me away from Catete. Even Petropolis is too far.

Obviously I did not speak of his daughter, though I confess that had I had an opportunity I should have spoken ill of her, with the secret intention of inflaming his anger even more and making a reconciliation impossible. In this way she would not depart for the fazenda nor I lose the object of my observations. Yes, you may record this, my dear journal, because it is the pure, naked truth, and no one is going to read it. Should anyone do so they will consider me an evil person, but you lose nothing by appearing evil; in fact you gain almost as much as if you were.

Yesterday the father, today the daughter. With her I felt the urge to malign her father, so loud was she in praise of his action in freeing the slaves. An impulse which led to nothing: a pure whim. Instead I saw myself obliged to sing his praises too, which only encouraged her to amplify her own panegyric.

She declared that he was a good master, and they good slaves, and told of incidents when she was a girl and young woman so artlessly and earnestly that I felt the urge to seize her hand and kiss it as a sign of approbation. An impulse which led to nothing. Nothing happened this afternoon.

19 April

The Baron departed with his slaves' deed in his suitcase. Perhaps he had heard something of the Government's intention. It is said that when the Chambers meet a project will be presented. And high time too. I still remember what I read about us when I was overseas, on the occasion of Lincoln's famous proclamation: 'I, Abraham Lincoln, President of the United States of America . . .' More than one newspaper spoke openly of Brazil, saying it only remained for the last Christian nation to imitate him and put an end to slavery. I hope that today they give us due praise. It came late in the day, but it is the liberty that Tiradentes* and his fellow conspirators demanded.

7 May

Today the Ministry presented their proposal of abolition to the Chamber. It is straightforward abolition, and they say that within a few days it will be law.

13 May

It's law at last. I never was, neither would my official position allow me to be, an open advocate of abolition, but I confess to feeling enormous pleasure when I heard of the final vote in the Senate and the Regent's sanction. I was in Rua do Ouvidor, where there were celebrations and a great tumult.

An acquaintance of mine from the press saw me there and offered me a place in his carriage, which was in Rua Nova, as he intended to join the procession organized to ride round the palace and salute the Regent. My head was in such a whirl that I very nearly accepted, but my retiring habits, my diplomatic training, my temperament and my age combined to restrain me

* a hero of the Brazilian independence movement

more effectively than the coachman's reins did his horses, and I refused. I did so with regret. I took my leave of him and the group who joined him, who then left together by way of Rua Primeiro de Março. They told me later that the demonstrators stood up in their carriages, which were open, and cheered loudly outside the palace, where all the Ministers were gathered too. Had I gone I should probably have done the same, and even now I wouldn't have been able to explain.... No, I wouldn't have done a thing: I'd have hidden my face between my knees.

Thank goodness we have done away with it. It was high time. Although we burn all the laws, decrees and instructions, we can never destroy all the private regulations, records and inventories, nor erase the institution from history or even from poetry. Poetry will speak of it, especially in those verses of Heine, which perpetuate our name. They record how the captain of a slave ship told of having left three hundred Negroes in Rio de Janeiro, where 'the House of Gonçalves Pereira' paid him a hundred ducats a head. It is of no consequence that the poet confuses the name of the buyer and calls him Gonzales Perreiro; it was the rhyme or his bad pronunciation that was to blame. Neither do we have ducats; but here it was the seller who transferred into his own language the currency of the buyer.

14 May

There is no public rejoicing can equal a deep personal satisfaction. This reflection came to me just now as I was leaving Flamengo, and I came to write down both it and the motive that prompted it.

It was the Aguiars' first at-home, a lively gathering with a fair number of guests. Rita didn't go; she asked me to explain that it was too far for her to travel and she didn't feel up to it. Our hosts seemed so happy that I attributed it not simply to having their friends around them, but also to the great event of the day. This is what I had in mind when I uttered one single word whose significance, spoken to Brazilians, should have been clear enough: 'Congratulations.'

'So you knew already?' they both asked.

Not understanding them I had no idea what to reply. What was it I was supposed to know already to congratulate them about, if not what was public knowledge? I put on one of my most engaging conciliatory smiles and waited, whereupon between them, speaking quickly, they informed me that the letter had come as a most welcome surprise. Not knowing what letter it was or who it was from, I limited myself to saying, 'Of course.'

'Tristão is in Lisbon,' concluded Aguiar. 'He's just got back from Italy, and is well, very well.'

I understood. That is how it is that amid the general rejoicing a source of personal joy can arise which takes precedence over all else. Far from blaming them for this I was in full agreement and pleased to see them so sincere. I supposed that their godson's letter, arriving after years of silence, was a compensation for the sadness he had left behind. Like the liberation of the slaves, the letter was long overdue, and though late, it had arrived safely. I congratulated them again with the air of one from whom no secrets are concealed.

16 May

Fidelia returned home with regrets on both sides. They are great friends, the old couple seeming to be her true parents, and she their daughter. The Judge, who told me this, repeated what his niece had said about the Aguiars, in particular Dona Carmo.

'It's not one of those flash-in-the-pan friendships,' he added. With her, as with them, it has developed slowly and is deep-rooted. They are capable of stealing my niece, and she of allowing herself to be stolen. Anyway, if it weren't them it would be her father. I think my brother is already weakening. The last time he wrote, after abusing the Emperor and the Princess, he did not forget to say 'he thanked her for her best wishes'. Fidelia hadn't sent him any best wishes, she was still in Flamengo; it was I who had invented them in my letter to see what effect they would produce. He's bound to weaken. Children, Counsellor, are the very devil. If anything were to happen to my Carlos I think it would kill me.'

I intend to stay indoors for four or five days, not to rest, because I don't do anything, but so as not to see or hear anyone except my man José. And him, if he obeys me, I'll send off on a fool's errand to Tijuca. I find there are more people annoy me than please me, yet I am aware that this proportion is entirely my fault, not theirs. What a wearisome business old age is.

Rita wrote asking for information about an auctioneer. She must be pulling my leg. What do I know about auctioneers or auctions? When I die they can sell off the little I shall leave privately, with or without a discount, and my own skin with it. It's not new, it's not beautiful, nor is it of superior quality, but it will always serve to make a drum or a rustic tambourine. There's no need to call in an auctioneer.

That's what I'll put in my reply to Rita, adding some bits of news that I picked up – Tristão's letter, for instance, the Baron's thanks to his daughter, and this great hoax, that Fidelia has consented to marry me. On second thoughts, no. If I tell her that she won't believe it; she'll burst out laughing and come straight over here. Just what I don't want. I need to be free from other people's company, even hers. I'll just say that the auctioneer is dead. He's probably still alive, but he has to die some day.

Yesterday I wrote to Rita to announce his demise and today, on opening the papers, I read of the death of the auctioneer Fernandes. His name was Fernandes, and he died of some disease or other. From all accounts he was an excellent paterfamilias and a respected, hardworking citizen. The *Vida Nova* referred to him as *great*, probably because he voted liberal.

On account of my letter and today's news Rita came running to see me. Women ought not to write letters; few say what they want to say clearly, and many express themselves inadequately or vaguely. Rita had inquired after the auctioneer, having been told that he lived in Catete and had fallen seriously ill some days ago. As he was my neighbour I might have some news of him.

That was the reason for her inquiry, but she had forgotten to mention it.

For a minute, no, not that, for a fleeting instant, I hesitated between confessing my fabrication or leaving it concealed by the coincidence. But Rita is my sister, and rather than be offended would end up laughing about it too. She heard my confession without showing annoyance, but neither did she laugh. The reason for this is unimportant and barely worth mentioning except to explain the letter and her solemnity. She had an account to settle with the deceased in respect of objects she had sent to be sold and, not knowing whether he had sold them or not, she was in doubt how to retrieve them or obtain the money. All she has to do is go to the warehouse, where there are bound to be records of everything. I promised to go there with her tomorrow. That pleased her and she began to smile, and later told me what the objects were – old pictures and novels she had read.

She stayed for dinner. Before sitting down we saw Fernandes's funeral procession pass by, and she took it into her head to count the carriages. Alas, I used to do so myself as a child, but it seems she has not lost her passion for statistics. Fernandes had thirty-seven or thirty-eight carriages.

I close the page at this point with the sole object of reminding myself that chance too can be a corrective to lies. The man who sets out lying shamelessly or furtively often ends up being punctilious and sincere.

22 May

On the way Rita told me what she knew about Tristão's letter and the reply that Dona Carmo had sent. She knows more than I do. Tristão was profuse in his apologies for his silence of many years, blaming it on work and other distractions. Recently, after graduating in medicine, he had gone on a study tour through many countries, but not being able to give an account of his travels he hoped one day to tell them all about it should he ever return to Rio. He asked for news of them both, also for their portraits, and sent them some engravings together with best wishes from his mother and father, who are still in Lisbon. It is a long, affectionate letter, full of tender memories. Dona

Carmo's reply, Rita said, is in a really motherly vein. Incapable of displaying her hurt feelings, she is all affection and forgiveness. She makes only one complaint, which is that when asking for portraits of her and her husband he neglected to send one of himself, the latest, since she still has all his earlier ones. She writes at great length, recalling his childhood and schooldays, ending by hinting that he should come to Rio to tell them about his travels. The engravings are by Goupil.

Rita was with her on the 15th, between one and two in the afternoon, after Fidelia had left to return to her uncle's. In spite of the girl's departure, and of missing her, Dona Carmo is delighted at the growing affection between the two of them, and equally so at the resurrection of her godson. She used the word resurrection imagining that the lad had forgotten them completely, but she now saw that this was not so and that he was no different from when he had left. Whether talking or silent, there were moments when Dona Carmo seemed heavy-hearted, and once Rita thought she saw a tear glistening in her eye, but it was just a tiny one.

23 May

Les morts vont vite. I had no sooner buried the auctioneer than I forgot all about him. That's why in my entry yesterday I omitted to mention that at Fernandes's warehouse we found Rita's objects duly accounted for, having been sold and the money accredited to the owner. It's not much, and she'll receive it in due course. There is no need to mention this, but at least it is good for the dead man's reputation.

One other thing that I forgot to mention too, and much more important since the auctioneer's calling may disappear one day, but the lover's will never wither and die. It was Rita's fault because instead of telling me right away, she only gave me the news as she was getting on the tram in Largo S. Francisco. It seems that Fidelia has made a conquest: those were her own words.

'Made a conquest?' I repeated, not understanding her right away.

'Yes, a young man has fallen for her.'

'There must be plenty of them,' I retorted.

She had no time to say more. She was already on the tram, which was about to leave. She pressed my hand, smiled and waved goodbye.

24 May, midday

This morning, as I was thinking of the young man who had been smitten by the widow's charms, the lady herself came to visit me and asked my advice on the matter. I found her in the living room, wearing her usual black dress with white trimmings. I sat her down on the sofa then, seated on the chair alongside, waited for her to speak.

'Tell me, Counsellor,' she said, lightly but seriously, 'what do you think I should do? Should I marry or remain a widow?'

'Neither one nor the other.'

'Don't jest, Counsellor.'

'I am not jesting, madam. Widowhood is unbecoming for such a young woman. Marriage yes, but to whom if not to me?'

'That is exactly the conclusion I had come to myself.'

I took her hands in mine. We gazed into each other's eyes, my own piercing her brow, her neck, the back of the sofa, the wall, until they finally came to rest on my servant, the only other person in my room, where I was lying in bed. From the street outside came the customary morning cry, 'Brushes-o! Dusters-o!'

To my amusement I realized it was just a dream. The street cries continued, while my man, José, apologized for having woken me, but it was gone nine o'clock, almost ten. I washed, had coffee and glanced through the papers. Some of these celebrated the anniversary of the Battle of Tuiuti. This brought to mind the occasion when, during my diplomatic days, the news of the battle arrived and I had had to give details to a group of foreign journalists anxious to learn the truth. Twenty more years and I shall no longer be here to recall the memory; another twenty and, apart from the odd one, there will be no survivors among either the journalists or the diplomats; yet another twenty, and no one at all. And the Earth will continue to revolve around the Sun with the same obedience to the laws that govern them, and the Battle of Tuiuti, like that of Thermopylae or Jena, will cry out from the depths of the abyss those words from Renan's prayer, 'O Abyss, Thou alone art God.'

A slight misconception ending up in despondency, and all to say little or nothing. With D. Francisco Manoel, I can say, 'By nature I am meticulous and long-winded; loneliness and melancholy, which feeds on itself . . . My page is full of contradictions, all fruit of a sexagenarian temper, disenchanted and insatiable. Well, perhaps not so insatiable nor all that disenchanted. Confidences to my journal, for my journal.

26 May

Here are the details of the fellow smitten by Noronha's widow. Twenty-eight years old, single, a lawyer with the Bank of Brazil, which explains his relationship with the Aguiars, good-looking, well-mannered, though somewhat timid. He's the son of a former landowner in the North, who now lives in Recife. He is said to be highly talented and to have a brilliant future. His name is Osorio.

He was there at Flamengo on the night of the 14th, the Aguiars' first at-home. I saw nothing to make me suspect the inclination he is now credited with, but it seems he was attracted to her then and his passion is increasing. Who knows, we may see a fiancé emerge, and Rita will lose the bet she made with me. Fidelia can quite easily marry without forgetting her first husband or betraying the affection she felt for him.

29 May

Yesterday at the Aguiars' gathering I was able to observe that the young lawyer has been badly smitten by Noronha's widow. There is no other explanation for the glances he throws at her, which are long and lingering. He is certainly timid, but it is a timidity mingled with respect and adoration. If we had a dance he might invite her for a quadrille, but I doubt he would ask her for a waltz. They chatted together at length on two occasions, and even then it was she who did most of the talking. Osorio spent most of the time gazing at her, and wisely so, since she

49

has an elegance which nevertheless is quite in keeping with the sobriety of her condition.

I too had a brief spell with her by the window. We both agreed that there is no bay in the world superior to that of our Rio de Janeiro.

'I haven't seen many,' she said, 'but I haven't seen one to equal it.'

We had many interesting things to say about this – at least she did – well, perhaps I did too. I wanted to ask her if in the seas she had crossed she had ever seen a fish like the one swimming round her now, but our intimacy has not reached that point, and politeness forbade. We spoke of the city and its attractions. She never goes to the theatre, of any kind, and knows nothing of plays or operas, so I did not pursue the subject. Inspired by the second part, the lyrical, I inquired about her piano playing, which I had heard so highly spoken of.

'That's just flattery on the part of my friends,' she said, with a smile.

Then she admitted that she has not played for a long time, and will likely end up forgetting what she knows. She was probably not sincere in this supposition, but modesty is always to be excused, and she seems to be modest. I led the conversation so as to be able to listen more than talk, and Fidelia did not decline this distribution of roles. She spoke little of herself but much of the Aguiars. On this subject she spoke with considerable warmth, and though she told me nothing new, what she felt for the two was spoken from the heart. She even said Dona Carmo was much like her mother, and occasionally reminded her of her – it might be simply the affection that she showed her. At all events, when we separated we were almost friends.

I did not tell the Aguiars what Fidelia had said about them, but when I spoke to Dona Carmo about the girl's musical gifts she confirmed Fidelia's intention never to play again. Otherwise she would have asked her to play something for us.

'One day her own love of music will persuade her to play again, at home, just to herself . . .' I replied.

'Maybe. In any case I shan't ask her to play here. Our applause might bring back memories; on the other hand if it took her mind off things it would lessen the pleasure she feels in mourning her husband. Don't you think she's an angel?'

I said I did. I'd have agreed she was even better than that had I been asked. Dona Carmo believes she will be reconciled with her father, but has no fear of losing her. Fidelia will be a daughter to both is the gist of what she said, omitting various details and the nature of the affection she feels for her. With regard to what she said about the 'pleasure of mourning her husband', I assume that Dona Carmo is one of those people for whom suffering is something divine.

End of May

Today is the last day of the month. May is usually celebrated in poetry as the month of flowers, though that can be said of the rest of the year. I found it difficult to accustom myself to the changes of season encountered in foreign parts.

Fidelia, on the other hand, to judge from what she said that night in Flamengo, and despite being born here and brought up in the country, found these changes delightful. There are people who seem to have been born in the wrong place, in a climate different from or the opposite to what they want, so that if they remove from the one to the other it is as if they are restored to where they belong. Such creatures are uncommon, but I never stated that Fidelia was common.

She gave me a lively and interesting description of her impressions abroad on the arrival of spring, and no less so of the ice-bound winter. I asked myself whether she was not destined to pass from ice to flowers through the agency of that young lawyer, Osorio. At this point I will register the blank that then took possession of my heart.

9 June

This is the first line I have written this month. Not for lack of subject matter, just the contrary. Nor was it lack of time. Lack of disposition, perhaps. Now it's back.

There is so much to say. In the first place, Osorio received a letter from his father asking him to visit him without delay as he is seriously ill. Osorio made his preparations and embarked for

Recife. Not right away, however, for it seems that Fidelia's image kept him here for three days, either because he couldn't drag himself away from her, or for fear of her falling into someone else's hands, or for both reasons together.

It is very wrong of parents to fall sick, especially if they happen to be in Recife, or in any other city other than that in which their lovelorn sons live close to their ladies. We have a right to love, also to youth, and to prejudice either is virtually a crime. If I had been able to tell this to Osorio he might not have left; he would have found that my observations echoed his own feelings and written a sympathetic letter to his father. But no one told him.

Another means to reconcile his sympathy and his love would be to write to Fidelia, telling of his departure and asking for a few minutes of her time. Such a letter, if sufficiently frank, would naturally arouse the widow's curiosity, and the presence or otherwise of the Judge at the interview would be of no consequence. Perhaps he would prefer to leave the room.

'You can stay here, uncle,' she would say, on receiving Osorio's visiting card.

'No, I'd better leave. It's probably some legal matter,' he would reply, smiling, 'and since I'm a magistrate I ought not to hear anything now as it will come up before me later.'

Osorio would come in, and after the usual greeting would ask for the widow's hand. Supposing that she refused, she would do so politely, almost with affection, declaring apologetically that she had decided never to marry again. There would be a long pause, and the rest can be imagined. Osorio might perhaps ask if that was her last word, and to curtail the interview she would incline her head, and he would leave. Fidelia would then run to give the news to her uncle. I like to think that he would support the lawyer's suit, recounting his good qualities, his prosperous career, his distinguished family and all the rest of it. Fidelia would not repent of her refusal.

'I have decided never to marry again,' she would say for the third time that afternoon.

Peter denied Christ three times before the cock crew. Here there would be no cock, but dinner, and shortly afterwards the two would go to the table. For the first few minutes they would say nothing, he thinking of the advantages of his niece marrying the lad, and she reflecting on the love he had expressed for her. No matter how firm the refusal, to have inspired such a passion always leaves a pleasant glow. A lady once told me this, I don't remember in what language, but that was the sense of it. And Fidelia would leave the table, without weeping as Peter did after the crowing of the cock.

All my own imaginings. The only true fact is that Osorio embarked, and off he has gone leaving the widow here no less charming than before, and to me much more so every day. I was with her today, and if I did not seize her and carry her off it was not for lack of strength or desire. I wanted to ask whether she had dreamed of the dismissed suitor, but the intimacy I am beginning to win does not permit such inquiries, nor would she tell me anything herself. What she did tell me was that she will soon be reconciled with her father, even if that means going to the fazenda. I naturally expressed my approval. Fidelia said that in his last letter to his brother her father had sent his regards, not by name, but collectively, 'my regards to everyone'.

'It must cost a lot for him to make the first move, but it doesn't worry me to do so,' she concluded.

'Naturally.'

'It was impossible to prevent our estrangement. Counsellor, you who have lived abroad for the greater part of your life can have no idea what these local animosities are like. My father is the kindest of men, but he never forgives an opponent. Now I think it's all over and done with – abolition has made him discontented with politics. He has already warned the Conservative leaders here not to count on him any longer for anything. If it was local quarrels that brought about our estrangement, I believe that he suffered as much as my husband and I.'

As proof of how they had both suffered she recounted several incidents in their married life, which I listened to with great interest. To record them here would take up too much space, so I'll mention only one.

Just over a year after their marriage they had the idea of proposing a reconciliation between the two families. First her husband would write to his father, and if he was willing, she would write to hers and they would wait for the second answer. Her husband's letter told of their happiness and their hopes for the future, and concluded by asking for his blessing or at least an end to his hostility. It was a long, friendly letter, full of the tenderest affection.

'My husband never showed me his father's reply,' said Fidelia. 'On the contrary, he told me that he had never received one. It was I who found it six or seven months after his death among his papers, and I realized why he had concealed it from me. . . .'

At this point she stopped. Being curious to know what was in it I evoked my diplomatic muse and prompted my new friend to a full disclosure or rectification by saying to her: 'Whatever he said about you or your father, it would be natural for an enemy. . . .'

'Oh no, it was nothing like that,' interrupted Fidelia. 'There was not a single offensive word. I hardly like to repeat what he said, just a line or a line and a half which went like this: "I received your letter but not your prescription for my rheumatism." That's all. He suffered from rheumatism and my husband, as you know, was a doctor.'

I chuckled to myself. I had not anticipated such wit from Paraiba do Sul, and at the same time I understood her husband's discretion. No less did I understand the widow's confession, giving way to the need to tell something which would allot to the father-in-law much of the blame that attached to the father. She could not silence the old man's blood in her. It was pure Santa-Pia.

14 June

Bad news of Santa-Pia. The Baron has a cerebral congestion, and Fidelia and her uncle are going to the fazenda tomorrow. It is not easy to guess what will come of all this, but there would be no difficulty in inventing something that will never happen. I could fill my journal with it and offer an illusory consolation. It is better merely to say that the reconciliation is likely to come about more quickly than expected, and in sadder circumstances.

Life offers unexpected parallels. Osorio's father's illness summoned the son to Recife, while that of Fidelia's father called the daughter to Paraiba do Sul. If this were a novel some critic would condemn such a coincidence as incredible, but as the poet tells us, the truth is frequently incredible. Today I shall go to the Aguiars' house to see if the old couple are missing their adopted daughter; no doubt they are.

Yes, they are missing her very badly. I found them alone and we talked about Fidelia. It is not so much her absence that saddens them as the sadness that she took away with her. What I mean is that what pained them was the grief she felt; that is what it seemed to me. They don't expect her to be away long and she will be able to come to Rio from time to time. In any case she is not so far off as to prevent them making a quick visit to the fazenda. Those were their hopes and feelings as far as I could gather. They told me of the shock it had been for the girl. Dona Carmo said I wouldn't believe how distressed she had found her.

'I offered to go with her to the fazenda. She thanked me, but refused, and for the first time called me by the name that heaven decreed I should never bear in this world. "Thank you little mother", she said, and gave me a warm kiss.'

I am not a particularly emotional man, nor unemotional either, but I understood the old lady's feelings and was pleased that at such a solemn moment Fidelia had spoken those tender words. She was much affected by it, and her husband too. Aguiar himself listened to his wife's account in silence, his eyes fixed on the ceiling. Naturally he did not want to be accused of weakness, but if weakness it was, it was revealed in his gestures: he got up, then he sat down; he lit a cigar, then changed the position of a vase. To dispel the atmosphere of gloom I inquired if the Baron's affairs were going well, and whether the freed slaves . . . Aguiar became a bank manager once more and gave me some advice on coffee planting and investments.

Just then a friend of theirs arrived and he also talked about Santa-Pia. He said that despite his losses things were not going too badly: he must have about three hundred contos. Aguiar can't say for sure, but he thinks that is about right.

'He has just the one daughter,' concluded the visitor, 'and it is likely she will marry again.'

Out of politeness to my hosts I was tempted to say that I didn't think so, but this laudable habit I have of keeping my mouth shut made me swallow the observation, and now I confess I am sorry.

In the end I have come to accept the idea of the lady's eternal widowhood, unless it be that this is due to jealousy or envy at seeing her married to another. It seems to me that Fidelia will really end up by not marrying, not just on account of loyalty to her late husband, but also because of her interests, which are in intellectual and artistic matters, and little or nothing else. This is between you and me, dear journal, to whom I confide everything I think, and everything I don't think.

17 June

The Baron of Santa-Pia is in a bad way.

18 June

Three cheers for Fortune, who occasionally rewards us for bitter sorrow with some unexpected consolation. The Aguiars received a letter from Tristão telling them he is embarking for Brazil, perhaps in the next steamer. As soon as I walked in . . . It was their at-home day, and I learned later that they had considered postponing it on account of Fidelia's distress, but then considering that it was a modest, unpretentious gathering, with no dancing and only rarely singing, just conversation and tea, they decided they could go ahead without giving offence.

As soon as I walked in Aguiar gave me the news. I paid my respects to Dona Carmo and congratulated her on the young man's coming, which she listened to with obvious pleasure. Half an hour later she and I took up the subject again. It was she who began, telling me that she was at home, never suspecting any such thing, when suddenly she saw a messenger from the bank come into the garden with a note from Aguiar giving her the good news, and enclosing the letter which Tristão

56

had addressed to them both. Giving me all these details, no doubt dispensable, Dona Carmo naturally wished to communicate her own excitement. I am familiar with such designs, at the same time secretive and avowed, an old vice of those who are happy.

Since the few people present were all close friends, by the end of the evening we were all encouraged to talk about the forthcoming guest. So here he is, on his way home, the godson they had considered forgetful of them, almost thankless, the half-son they had loved and helped to bring up. Aguiar and his wife replied to questions and recounted episodes of his childhood, stories of his good humour and cleverness, as well as some of his pranks, for children's pranks are only irritating at the time, in recollection they delight us, as do other things long past. One of the ladies present began to talk of some of Dona Carmo's acts of kindness towards the child, but the old lady quickly changed the subject so that we only heard of one or two. A family evening. I left early and came home to drink some milk, write this and go to bed. Till another day, journal.

20 June

Telegram from Paraiba do Sul: 'Baron Santa-Pia passed away this morning.' I'll write to Rita with the news and send cards of condolence. Should I do the same with the Aguiars? Condolence no, just a polite, informal visit tomorrow or the next day . . .

21 June

Aguiar is going to Santa-Pia fazenda to express his condolences to Fidelia, and leaves tomorrow. Dona Carmo is staying. That's what he told me in Rua Ouvidor.

'I've already sent mine,' I told him. 'Please accept them too if the affection between you and Dona Fidelia justifies such participation in her grief. . . .'

'We both share the sorrow that afflicts our dear friend. Carmo wished to go with me, but I said no, she ought not to go. A hasty journey like that would be too tiring for her.'

So Aguiar goes off to lessen his joy in his son in the grief of the daughter, and will return to find consolation for the girl's sorrow in the happiness of the young man. Everything finds its compensation in this world, thank goodness. The trouble is that they are not a true son and daughter, but only linked by affection, and for lack of their own children the Aguiars console themselves with these. Yet it often happens that the true ones prove to be less true.

Rita called here today. She was on her way to visit the Aguiars, but I suggested she go with me tomorrow and she agreed.

Rita and I called to see Dona Carmo yesterday. I left earlier than I intended; if possible I would have stayed longer.

We found her half happy, half sad, if such an expression can define a state of mind which defies description, at least by me. She greeted us in her usual manner, her words and gestures having an unaffected warmth that is quite delightful. When we mentioned Fidelia she spoke of her friend's sorrow with corresponding sorrow of her own, and she referred to her husband's departure the previous morning without a word of the commitments he had had to break. Before long, however, when we asked after her godson, her answers were much more cheerful. The remainder of our visit was divided between the two, but naturally the greater part of the conversation was devoted to the young man since his absence had been longer, the distance greater and his return so unexpected.

Dona Carmo resumed her account of the other evening which, we being but three, was now more intimate. She wouldn't describe the whole of his early childhood, as she admitted time was too short, but she gave us the essentials. He was a sickly child, delicate and painfully thin. She did not actually say that she mothered him, she is incapable of giving credit to herself, but I knew she did, and could perceive from her tender references to him that that was how it was. Rita ventured to say, with a laugh, 'Children don't realize the trouble they give, and what little they do they soon forget.'

'But you have to forgive Tristão what is natural in a young man,' returned Dona Carmo. 'He's not really bad; he forgot about us for a while, but his age and the novelty of his surroundings explain everything. The proof is that he is on his way to see us, and if you read his letters. . . . Did Aguiar show you his last?'

'No,' I replied. 'He just told us what he said.'

I think she would have liked to show me the lad's letters, or perhaps just one, a passage or a line, but for fear of boring us she dismissed the idea. That is how it seemed to me, and I note it here. We returned to the widow, then back again to Tristão, and she only passed on to a third subject because politeness demanded. But out of respect for her deepest desires I brought the conversation back once more to her adopted children, this being my way of showing courtesy to the old lady. I must say I left there quite enchanted with her, as did my sister.

In the street Rita said: 'There are few creatures like her.'

'So I believe. So I believe. She is admirable . . . with no disparagement to you.'

'Me?' replied Rita, hastily. 'I don't consider myself a bad person, but I'm a long way from being like her. You know, everything about her is good, even her opinions, which aren't always right because she pardons and excuses everyone. I'm not like that: in my opinion many people are bad, and if I'm called upon to say so I'm not afraid to speak out. Dona Carmo is incapable of criticizing anyone. The most she will do is to find an explanation or just say nothing at all.'

24 June

Yesterday I chatted to Senhora Aguiar about the old-time celebrations on the nights of St John, St Anthony and St Peter, with the bonfires and telling of fortunes. Dona Carmo seized on the subject to bring up her godson again. To the devil with the fellow. It's her daughter who at this moment must be feeling sad there on the fazenda where no doubt as a trusting, credulous girl she must have spent many a St John's Night. Tonight must be depressing for her with no father or mother, and no husband to take their place. An uncle is but a poor substitute for these.

I too had my fortune read long ago. All that was needed to see into the future was a book, a set of rhyming quatrains and a couple of dice. The title of the page might say, for example, 'To know if you will marry the person you love'. Then you took the dice and threw, say, five and two, making seven. You found the seventh quatrain and read it. Now suppose it said . . . Enough, I've crossed out the quatrain I actually wrote here. Usually they were just amusing, but also made fun of the person whose fortune was being told. Everybody laughed. There were some who actually believed in it, but in any case it passed the time until sleep overtook us. And then along would come that old servant of mankind, whom the pagans called Morpheus, who closes the eyes of pagans, Christians and even unbelievers with his eternal leaden fingers. And now sleep, my good friend, you will come creeping on me in an hour or two without the help of either dice or books of fortunes. If anything you will bring dreams, but not the same as those of long ago.

27 June

Mass for Baron Santa-Pia in São Francisco de Paula Church. The Judge's son represented the family; he and his niece heard mass at the fazenda. That also must have brought back memories for the widow. The fazenda has a chapel where a priest said mass on Sundays and heard confession in Lent. That was the custom when I was a child, and I still remember how, at Lent, the other boys and I used to hide from the confessor under beds and in odd corners of the house. Even at that age we associated religious duties with the drudgeries of life and sought to escape them. However, the priest who heard my first confession was gentle, attentive, and guided me in my confession telling me those sins I had to mention, etc. He had my absolution on the tip of his tongue even before his ears had registered my sins, or so it seemed to me. May his memory forgive me if this is untrue. It was a long time ago. My second confession was when I got married. Since then I have remained virtuous.

There was quite a crowd in the São Francisco de Paula Church. In the sacristy were sheets of paper for those who attended to sign, and for one or two others who didn't go but got someone to sign for them. I saw judges, lawyers, businessmen, civil servants and ladies, any number of ladies. Some of these were girls, friends of Fidelia, others elderly, of her mother's time. One of these, merely a friend of the widow, was the one who would have turned up had no one else been present – Senhora Aguiar of course. Rita was there too, and later had lunch with me.

If masses could be said according to the occasion, I would say the priest adapted his to the limited presence of the deceased's family, so short it was. But it is not like that: each priest says mass in his normal manner, hastily or leisurely, as he is accustomed to read or speak.

30 June

Well now, Fidelia has sent Dona Carmo a letter which is a psychological treatise, a veritable portrait of the soul. As they had the kindness to show it to me I was prepared to find it interesting even before reading it, but having read it my good intention was unnecessary: I did find it interesting, and said so, re-reading several passages. There were no clichés or high-sounding phrases; as a letter it is simply simple, if the adverb can go with the adjective, which I suppose it can, at least for me.

There were only four pages, not the type of writing paper that we use, but the old-fashioned variety known as heavyweight, of a brand called Bath that her father used on the fazenda. She writes at length about him and her feelings at being there again, the memories aroused by the walls of the bedrooms and living rooms, the columns of the veranda, the stones of the well, the old windows, the rustic chapel. And amongst these fleeting memories she has a few words for the slave women and the urchins whom she left small and now finds grown up and who, now freed, retain the same affection they had when slaves. Among the ghosts of the past is the image of her mother beside her father and, both near and far off, in the rooms and in a corner of her heart, that of her husband, so vivid I felt I could see it, and it seemed to me imperishable.

I am coming to realize that this girl is an even finer person than I had originally thought. It is not a question of whether or not she loves her husband; I believe that although she loves him this constancy cannot add to the purity of her feelings. This is due either to him, to her, or to both together. What most impresses me about her, apart from her simple, spontaneous reaction to things, are the observations and conclusions she draws from them. In this there may be some exaggeration on my part, but I think not. Had it been the beginning of the year I might have said this was just the fancy of a disillusioned old lover cheering his solitude by confiding his admiration to his journal. But that is not the case; it is just his old temperament having a last fling. Now all I have left is aesthetic appreciation, if that, and in this respect it is true that I find the widow extremely attractive, but only when she is present before my eyes. She really is a handsome woman, with a rare gift of self-expression. And her letter adds that final touch of spirituality.

I believe that Dona Carmo's feelings about her are the same as mine, but on this occasion what affected her most deeply was her final greeting, the last three words before the very last, which is her name: 'Your loving daughter, Fidelia.' I realized this on seeing her glance down three or four times to the bottom of the sheet, unwilling to finish folding it and to put it away.

1 July

Happiness sometimes comes in gales that carry all before them. Yesterday the Aguiars received Fidelia's letter, and today brought another from Tristão announcing his embarkation in an English steamer, due to arrive on the 23rd or 24th. Naturally their joy on receiving this news knew no bounds: with Fidelia here, and calling herself the old lady's daughter, and Tristão on his way, telling them that this letter is his last, and will shortly be followed by himself. All this happening at the same time!

They are preparing him accommodation in the house. Aguiar is so delighted that, contrary to his usually discreet habits, he already has in mind the furniture he will get for his bedroom. It is simple but elegant. Probably his wife has already begun work on the wool and linen coverings for the table and chairs. He didn't tell me this, nor did anyone else. It was I who guessed it, and I note it down to convince myself of what is easily observed. For the good old lady embroidery, sewing, in short all household work, was her manner of expressing her love. She sewed with her heart.

It is an old saying, I believe, or if not we can make it a new one, that things are only well done when they are done with love. It must be an old one, it seems so commonplace and so apt. It explains the perfection found in all her household activities. Like sleeping or breathing. This is not to detract from her merit: no matter how great the necessity, the virtue is no less. I too performed my diplomatic duties with love, and according to some Ministers well, but in my case (as distinct from Dona Carmo's) love and necessity were not enough, and had it not been for the career offered by the diplomatic service, it is likely that I should have ended up a judge, a banker or something else.

2 July

When Aguiar spoke to me yesterday we were in the Do Sul Bank, where I had gone to deposit some shares. I forgot to mention that on leaving I met Judge Campos near Candelaria Church. He had arrived from Santa-Pia the evening of the day before yesterday, and was on his way to the bank with some messages from his niece to the Aguiars. I asked if Fidelia intended staying there for good, but he said no.

'She won't stay there for good, just a few weeks, then she'll come back here and probably sell the fazenda, which I don't think is a bad idea. From what she said, if it would do any good she would stay on, but she feels the fazenda is too run down and she hasn't the strength to set it on its feet again. So she had the idea of selling up and coming to live with me. If she stayed on she'd manage. She took charge of everything herself and directed the work. She has the energy, the will-power and the authority. The freed slaves are working well.'

We talked a little more about the effects of abolition, and then parted.

5 July

I had promised to spend the evening with the broker, Miranda, and went there today. He has just returned from spending a few months in Europe, much fatter and as hot-headed as ever, but a good sort and an excellent husband. He had nothing new to report except a game, seemingly invented in the United States, and which he learned on board ship. It was unknown in my time, and is called poker. I introduced whist, which I still play, but I never gave up my old *voltarete*. But it seems poker will carry all before it. In Miranda's house even his wife plays.

His daughters don't play, neither does his sister-in-law, Dona Cesaria, who finds no pleasure in cards. She admitted (laughing) that there is more fun in talking scandal, which she does with great charm. This is what her husband lacks, though possessed of all other virtues. I sensed that the two were at loggerheads with the broker, not formally, because Dona Cesaria never quarrels outright, only sulks, but I felt they were annoyed when the broker embarked for Europe with his family. Whether they were or not, on their return they were reconciled. That is one of the lady's talents. Perhaps she had repeated gossip about her own sister or her brother-in-law, but she smoothed matters over so skilfully that I found them a united family. What she will say about me I have no idea, but I find her interesting and I prefer her tongue to poker – with the tongue you don't lose money.

When they discussed the death of Baron Santa-Pia and the situation of his daughter, Dona Cesaria wanted to know whether she would really marry again. It seems she has doubts concerning Fidelia's continuing widowhood. I did not say that I had come to the same conclusion, but held my tongue and said nothing. I had no wish to bring the other into the conversation, and how right I was! A little later Dona Cesaria accepted the hypothesis of Dona Fidelia's perpetual widowhood since she could find nothing good to say of her – no charm, no vivacity, no manners, nothing at all. She seemed to her quite lifeless. I smiled as expected, and went off to hear someone's exposition of the meaning of *bluff*. In poker, *bluff* is a kind of confidence trick.

13 July

Seven days without writing a single word, fact or observation, or I should say eight days, since today I still have nothing worthy of note. I'm only writing this so as not to lose the habit. It's not a bad habit to note down what one thinks and sees, and to do so even when you think and see nothing at all.

18 July

Tristão arrived in Pernambuco, and is expected here on the 23rd.

20 July

The Aguiars' godson arrived in Bahia. I think they are planning to give a welcoming party for him, albeit a modest one. His latest photograph has been framed and hung up. He's a fine-looking lad, and a certain air of arrogance in the photograph is not unbecoming, just the opposite.

25 July

Tristão has arrived. I haven't seen him yet, but then I haven't been outside the house these last three days. Amongst other things I've been tearing up old letters. It's nice to keep old letters, but since I'm old too and have no one to leave them to, it's better to tear them up. I kept just nine or ten to re-read some day before they share the same fate. None of them is worth a single one of Pliny's, but of all I can say the same as what he wrote to Apollinarius: 'We shall each have an equal share of pleasure: you in reading what I say, and I in saying it.' My Apollinariuses are all dead or old, the male and the female.

27 July

Today I saw Tristão coming down Rua Ouvidor with Aguiar; I guessed who it was from his portrait and his companion. His dress, though not differing from the usual Brazilian or Portuguese style, had a certain personal touch about it. Aguiar introduced us. Tristão conversed politely, showing a certain curiosity, I can't call it interest, in regard to me. Naturally he must have heard me spoken about at their house. We chatted for a mere five minutes, sufficient for him to tell me that he is delighted with what he has seen. I think he was sincere, because I love my native city in spite of its ancient, narrow streets, and also because I have travelled in foreign parts and used to speak in just that same way. However, this city is his too, and when I mentioned that having left Rio de Janeiro as a young lad he should not have forgotten it, he replied that that was quite right, he had forgotten nothing. His delight came exactly from that sensation of seeing things already known, a resurrection that was also a continuity, if I may so express what he told me in simpler terms than these.

He's a fine young man. Outspoken without being brash. His eyes are bright and alert, but maybe the brevity of our meeting was the cause of their having but this one expression; possibly on other occasions they are different. He is on the tall side and well built. I almost looked back at him when we were a short distance apart, but desisted in time; it would be hasty and indiscreet and perhaps not worth the trouble. I'll call at Flamengo one evening soon. I haven't been there for three weeks.

28 July

I have no doubt of Tristão's pleasure at seeing Rio de Janeiro again. Whatever the new customs and family ties, and however long the absence, the place where one spent one's childhood has always a special place in one's memory and one's heart. I believe he really is delighted, as he told me yesterday. Moreover, over there in Portugal he heard the same language as is spoken here, and his mother is that same Luisa, the Paulista who gave him birth, took him away with her, and is at present in Lisbon with his father, both of them now old.

I have never forgotten things I saw as a child. Even now I can remember two bearded fellows playing a carnival game. I must have been five years old, and they had wooden or metal basins, got themselves completely soaked and went home dripping with water. The only thing I don't remember is where they were. Another thing I remember too, although it was so many years ago, is the courtship of a young couple in the neighbourhood. Her name was Flor, she lived across the road and was very thin. He was thin too, but no one knew his name, he was only known to us by sight. He used to come in the afternoons and would walk from one end of the street to the other, three, four, five or even more times. Then one night we heard screams. The next morning I was told that the girl's father had ordered his slaves to give him a good beating. A few days later he was called up into the army, they say due to the influence of the girl's father.

Some believe that the beating was no more than a settlement of accounts for some reason connected with elections. It amounts to the same thing: love or elections, there is no lack of opportunity for discord between men.

What is the value of such recollections now, in this year of 1888? What use is the barber's shop that I remember seeing in those days, with leeches at the door inside a large glass jar full of water and some other peculiar stuff? It's ages since they gave up using leeches on the sick, yet here they are still swimming around in my brain as they did in the jars. The business was in the hands of barbers and chemists I think, but only the barbers did the blood-letting. Nowadays of course no one at all is bled. Customs and institutions, all alike come to an end.

31 July

Tristão has made a very favourable impression, and as proof that it is deserved it is sufficient to say that he doesn't displease me, just the contrary. He is polite, well-spoken and attentive, with neither affectation nor presumption, speaking modestly, yet giving his opinions with force and clarity. I have not heard him speak on important topics, nor would I expect this from one who has just arrived from abroad and is living with his family, but what I have heard has been interesting.

His dress and behaviour are like his conversation, revealing the same simplicity and good taste. The delight which he told me the other day he finds in Rio de Janeiro, he continues to find both in the city and in the inhabitants. He recognizes roads, houses, customs and people, asks questions about them and always shows interest in the replies he receives. Some things he recalls immediately, others after a brief explanation. In short, he is not a bad fellow.

For the Aguiars excellent is too inadequate a term to describe him. She is as enchanted as he is, even more so, and just in these few days has already taken him to various places. Judge Campos, who dined with them yesterday, told me that Dona Carmo is exactly like a child, hardly ever taking her eyes off her godson. Tristão is something of a musician, and that night, at her request, played a piece by Wagner which the Judge admired very much.

As well as Campos there was a Father Bessa at the dinner, the priest who baptized Tristão.

This priest was not known in Flamengo, and it was Tristão himself who discovered him, in a manner which is worthy of note. He made inquiries about him and, after a couple of days, learning that he lived in Praia Formosa, he announced his intention of going there, refusing his godfather's offer to accompany him.

'I want to go there on my own,' he replied, 'to show I have not forgotten my native city.'

So off he went, found his way there, and discovered the priest living in a miserable little hut. Bessa, who had been a guest at his parents' house, did not know him at first, but after a few words of introduction he remembered the old days and recognized the child he had baptized. Aguiar had expressed a wish to meet him and had told Tristão to invite him to his house whenever he wanted. He is a fine-looking old fellow, both as a man and a priest, the Judge said; although thin-faced and balding, he has retained an expression of serenity despite the wretched life he must have lived, even contriving to be cheerful.

1 August

The Judge also gave me news of his niece, who is well and will shortly be returning from the fazenda. She told him in a letter of a dream she had had recently in which she saw her father and her father-in-law in a bay, which might have been Rio de Janeiro. The two figures approached her hand in hand over the water and then stood in front of her on the beach. Death had reconciled them, so that never again would they be enemies, and they now recognized that worldly enmity is of no account, whether it be in politics or anything else.

I felt like telling the Judge that perhaps his niece had misunderstood them. Eternal reconciliation between two political enemies to my mind is more like eternal punishment. I know of nothing like it in the *Divine Comedy*. When God wishes to be Dante He is greater than Dante. I checked myself in time and bit back the jest. It would be like making mock of the girl's distress. I asked for more news of her and he complied, the main thing being that she is more determined than ever to sell Santa-Pia.

Aguiar showed me one of Fidelia's letters to Dona Carmo, fluently written in a firm, bold hand and with many expressions of affection. She promises to return to Rio soon. I am tired of hearing that she is coming soon, but have not yet tired of recording the fact in these idle pages. I term them such in order to contradict myself, having already referred to this journal as an admirable habit. After all one can maintain both opinions equally well, and in the long run it comes to the same thing. Idleness is an admirable habit.

Fidelia's letter begins with these three words: 'Dearest little mother', which left Dona Carmo in raptures of joy and tenderness – her husband's own words. Not everything is lost in banks, and if you do happen to lose money it merely changes hands.

Today is the anniversary of Ferraz's Ministry, and I wonder who still thinks of him or his fellow Ministers, some now dead, some grown old and others retired. It was he who, to my surprise and without my having asked, promoted me to Legation Secretary.

I was telling this to Aguiar, who replied with some of the political gossip of those days (1859–61), told with high spirits but no feeling of nostalgia. Aguiar is not cut out for public life; he is a family man, a husband, and now on top of that he also has children, his two 'adopted' children, Tristão more than Fidelia, for reasons I think I have already mentioned. He confirmed the Judge's good impressions of the young man and concluded, saying, 'Counsellor, you have already spoken to Tristão, listened to him, and I believe you have a good opinion of him, but I should like you to get to know him better. He speaks of you with great respect and admiration. He tells me that he saw you one day in Brussels, never dreaming that he would come to find you here and talk to you.'

'That's what he told me. I consider him an admirable young man.'

'He is, isn't he? That's what we think, and other people too. I didn't ask him to tell me about his life in Portugal, but I led the conversation so that he in fact told me a great deal about his studies, his travels and his acquaintances. He might have made some of it up, or exaggerated a little, but I don't think so. Everything he said sounds reasonable and tallies well with what we've seen of him here and know of his mother and father. If we could persuade him to stay with us for good, we would. But it's not possible. He came to stay just four months, but at our request he will stay two more. And I have hopes of being able to keep him nine or ten.'

'Did he come solely to visit you?'

'That's what he said. Maybe his father took advantage of him coming here and asked him to attend to some matters for him. Although he sold out everything he still has some interests here, but I didn't ask.'

'Well, see if you can make him stay longer. He'll end up staying here for good.'

4 August

On boarding the ferry for Niteroi whom should I find leaning against the rail but Tristão himself. He was gazing at the entrance to the bay as if his sole desire was to venture forth and sail across to Europe. I said this to him jokingly, but he denied it.

'I was admiring the beauty of this landscape of ours,' he explained.

'It is more beautiful over here.'

'It's much the same,' he said. 'I've seen everything here, and from the little I've seen abroad I still think this is the most magnificent view in the world.'

It was a well-worn topic, but a good conversational gambit. We made use of it and arrived at the landing stage after a lively exchange of ideas and opinions. I confess that mine were no newer than the original topic, and given in few words, whereas his had the advantage of evoking memories and anecdotes. I will not write everything he told me about his childhood and adolescent years, nor his youth spent in Europe. It was interesting of course, and seemed factually correct and sincere, but no matter how short the ferry crossing it was awfully long. We finally arrived at Praia Grande. When I told him that I preferred that name to the official administrative and political one of Niteroi, he disagreed. I replied that our disagreement arose from the fact that I was old and he young. 'I was brought up calling it Praia Grande. When you were born the name Niteroi was just catching on.'

There was nothing particularly witty about this remark, but he seemed to think so for he replied with a smile, 'Yours is a mind that will never grow old.'

'You think so?' I asked, incredulously.

'That's what my godparents said, and I see that they were telling the truth.'

I bowed my head in thanks and held out my hand: 'I'm going to the presidential palace. Until our return, we may meet then.'

An hour later, when I arrived back at the landing stage, I found him there. I supposed he had been waiting for me, but it was not for me to inquire nor probably for him to say so. The ferry drew near, came alongside and we boarded. On the return trip I learned something I did not know: Tristão, nicknamed "Brazilian" in Lisbon, like others of that country who return there from here, is a naturalized Portuguese citizen.

'Does Aguiar know?'

'Yes, he knows. What he doesn't know, but soon will, is that just before leaving I accepted an offer to go into politics and am going to be elected deputy next year. If it weren't for that I'd stay here with him and go and fetch my mother and father. I know he will try to dissuade me; he doesn't like politics, particularly when one is actively involved, but the decisive argument is my own liking for it and the agreement I made with the party leaders. I wrote for a time for a Lisbon newspaper, it's said not too badly. I've also spoken at party meetings.'

'They are very fond of you.'

'I know, just like a son.'

'There is also a girl who is like a daughter to them.'

'So I believe – a widow, the daughter of a farmer who died a short time ago. They spoke to me about her, and I've seen her photograph that my godmother framed herself. If you know my godmother you will know what a tender heart she has. She is everyone's mother. Her affection extends even to animals. Did they ever tell you about a third child they had which they were very fond of?'

'I don't think so. I don't remember.'

'It was a dog, just an ordinary little dog. It was in my time. A friend of my godfather's took it there one day when it was only a few months old, and they both fell in love with it. I won't tell you everything my godmother did for it, from feeding it on milk to making woollen coats and all the rest of it. Even if I had the time you wouldn't believe me. Not that it was anything extravagant or excessive, but it was all done so naturally and with such genuine care that it was as if the animal were a human being. It lived the usual ten or eleven years, had a nurse when it fell ill and caused tears to be shed when it died. As you enter the garden look to the left beside the wall, that's where they buried it. I had forgotten about it but my godmother pointed it out yesterday.'

I wasn't greatly impressed by this combination of bank manager and father to a dog, though it is true that Tristão stressed more the part played by Dona Carmo, who is a woman. From our previous meetings and these two ferry trips together, I feel that I understand the young man much better. I only heard him speak half a dozen words which might be taken as self-praise, and even then they were very modest. 'They say I don't write too badly' suggests his conviction that he writes well; but he didn't say so, and it might well be true.

7 August

Dona Carmo went to Nova Friburgo with her godson to show him the city where she was born, also, I think, the road and the very house itself. They say everything there is old-fashioned and peaceful. This accords well with her own habits for she has a taste for keeping old things, mementos of the past, as if they perpetuated her own youth. Tristão, not having the same interest, was nevertheless happy to accompany her. Everyone continues to like him, Campos most of all because he knew him as a boy. My sister Rita has barely seen him as she has been ill in bed. She got up the day before yesterday, and as I only heard about it yesterday I went to visit her. I gave her all the news of her friends' house and the Judge's, and encouraged her to visit the Aguiars herself when the two return from Nova Friburgo.

10 August

Poor old bumbling Aires, why on earth did you celebrate Ferraz's Ministry on the 3rd when it is on the 10th? The anniversary is today, old chap. You see what a good thing it is to go on noting down everything that happens. If you didn't you'd remember nothing or else get everything mixed up.

Fidelia arrives from Paraiba do Sul on the 15th or 16th. It seems the freed slaves are going to be disappointed: when they heard she was going to sell the fazenda they begged her not to do so or else to bring them all to Rio with her. That just shows you what it is to be beautiful and to have the gift of enslaving others. From this kind of slavery there are no laws or decrees that can free you, for the bonds are divine and everlasting. It would be funny to see her arrive in Rio with all her slaves; what could they do and how could she maintain them? It was difficult for her to make the poor devils understand that they have to work and that here there would be no work for them. What she did was to promise that she would never forget them, and should she never return to the fazenda, to recommend them to the new owner of the property.

11 August

Today I received a note from Tristão, written from Nova Friburgo, in which he says how delighted he is with all he has seen and heard. He remembered the city and finds both it and the inhabitants charming, and his companion even more so. I quote from his letter: 'My godmother, or mother – I don't know which to call her as both titles are correct – is most affectionately remembered here, not only by two old friends remaining from her childhood days, but also by others who knew her after she married, friends of the former or simply friends themselves. I like

73

the place and the climate; the temperature is ideal. We intend to stay another three days.'

There is nothing in the letter that couldn't be told on his return seeing that he is coming back in three days' time. I think he just wanted me to have something from him in writing, and to receive something in return. A question of mutual sympathy and attraction. I'll reply with a couple of lines.

... I've sent off the letter. I wrote thirty or so lines, in a friendly vein, making the news as cheerful as I could. I agreed that Nova Friburgo was delightful and ended up with these words: 'Come and have lunch with me when you get back and we'll exchange news.'

17 August

Fidelia has come back, Tristão has come back, everyone has come back, and I myself have come to my senses – or in other words, I am reconciled to my white hairs. The looks I cast at Noronha's widow were those of pure admiration, with no other intention whatsoever, not as at the beginning of the year. True, at that time I used to quote that verse of Shelley's, but it is one thing to quote verses and quite another to believe in them. A short time ago I read a most pious sonnet written by a young atheist who needed to keep well in with a wealthy, religious uncle. So although at that time I didn't entirely believe the English poet, I do now, and I repeat what I've just said for my own benefit. Admiration is quite enough.

19 August

Tristão came to lunch. The first part of the lunch was a commentary on the letter he sent me. He told me how as a child his godmother had taken him several times to Nova Friburgo, maybe it was three times. He remembered the city and liked it very much. He sang the praises of Dona Carmo, saying that her affection, her warmth and good-heartedness make her a very special, very singular person, because such qualities are themselves singular and rare. He recounted stories of long ago and celebrated love affairs. Then he said that these impressions of our country revived memories of his

74

early childhood and adolescence. The latter part of the meal was devoted to his naturalization and politics. Politics seem to mean a great deal to him. He spoke at length of present developments in Portugal and Spain, and of his own ideas and ambitions as a servant of the State. He did not actually use these last four words, but those he did use came to the same thing. Despite some exaggeration the subject was interesting and he speaks well.

Before leaving he returned to the subject of Rio de Janeiro, and he also spoke about Recife and Bahia, but his main theme was Rio.

'One never forgets the place where one was born,' he concluded, with a sigh.

Perhaps this was intended as an apology for his naturalization, a way of saying he was still Brazilian. I went one step further, claiming that the adoption of another nationality was a political act, frequently a duty imposed on one, but which does not erase one's feelings for one's origins or memories of infancy. My choice of words delighted him, or maybe it was my tone of voice and the special winning smile I gave. Or all together. Whatever it was, he nodded his head in agreement several times, and his farewell handshake was firm and prolonged.

Until here a touch of censure. Now a measure of justice.

His age, the presence of his parents, who live there, the companionship of the other medical students, the same language, the same customs, all these go to explain his adoption of a new country. If we add a career in politics, a glimpse of power, the urge to win fame, the first steps towards a long-cherished ambition, I find it normal and natural that Tristão should exchange one country for the other. I believe him to be well-meaning, and I understand the emotions that here, his own homeland excites without weakening the new links already forged.

21 August

The day before yesterday I left my visiting card for Fidelia, and yesterday, on the invitation of her uncle, whom I met in the street, I went to have tea with them.

Naturally we talked about her late father. Fidelia spoke at length of her experiences during his last days, but did not mention the estrangement caused by her marriage, this being old history, now forgotten. The blame, if there was blame, was shared between them: she for falling in love with another, and he for his malevolence towards the man of her choice. That is my opinion, not hers, for her sorrow is that of the daughter and the widow, and if she had to choose again between her father and her husband she would choose the husband. She also spoke about the fazenda and the freed slaves, but seeing that the subject was becoming too personal she switched the conversation and we discussed the city and the events of the day.

Shortly afterwards Dona Cesaria and her husband, Dr Faria, arrived to pay their respects. The warmth with which Dona Cesaria spoke to Fidelia, and her welcoming kiss, in my opinion made up for the backbiting she had indulged in days before in Miranda's house. On that occasion, despite her witty manner, I did not like to see the widow so slighted, and now all is well again. I repeat what I said earlier on, the lady has much more charm than her husband, which is not saying much. When he runs other people down he does so clumsily; she is always entertaining.

Dona Cesaria made up for everything. It was not so much the words of praise and friendship she used yesterday, but the look in her eyes, her expression of admiration and approval, her fixed, almost unchanging smile, all this showed the extent of her affection. Paper money is money just the same. With it I bought this pen and ink, the cigar I am smoking and the lunch I am beginning to digest. No comparison is possible between the two ladies, but as far as conversation goes Dona Cesaria alone is more than enough. In my life I have met several such people who can make a bore sound interesting and stir a corpse to life. They project themselves into everything. Fidelia seems to get on well with her and listens to her with pleasure. It was a pleasant evening.

I was forgetting one thing. Fidelia had the photographs of her father and husband framed together and placed in the living room. She never did this during the Baron's lifetime out of respect to his feelings, but now that death has reconciled them she does so too in effigy. She gave me this explanation herself while I was looking at them. Neither her former delicacy nor her present determination surprises me; it is in keeping with the nature of the person.

When I said this outside to the Farias (we left together), the husband turned up his nose. I did not see the gesture itself, but the one word he spoke implied it; it was, 'Affectation!' I was going to say that that was impossible in such a private and intimate matter, but I held my tongue. Dona Cesaria neither approved nor disapproved of what he said; she merely observed that the gaslight was dim. I found it very bright, so I assumed it was the easiest way for her to change the subject. His wife's words gave Faria an opportunity to run down the gas company and the Government, and he declared that the authorities were thieves. It was eleven o'clock.

5 p.m.

I don't want to close the day without saying that I feel my eyes tired, perhaps there may be something wrong with them, and I don't know whether I shall continue this record of events, impressions and ideas. Perhaps it would be better to stop. Old age needs a rest. I have enough to do writing letters in reply to those I receive, as well as a job the Foreign Office asked me to do some days ago – now fortunately completed.

24 August

What, interrupt my journal? Never! Here I am once again, pen in hand. To be honest I find a certain pleasure in putting on to paper all those memories and reflections that seem to want to flow from one's head. Let's get down to current observations.

What brings the pen to my hand this time is the shadow of the shadow of a tear.

I think I saw it the day before yesterday (the 22nd) on Fidelia's eyelash when I referred to the estrangement between her father and her husband. I have no desire to remember it now. I wish I had never seen it, or so much as suspected its existence. I don't like tears, even in the eyes of women, beautiful or otherwise; they are an admission of weakness and I was born with a distaste for the weak. After all, women are less weak than men – or more patient, more able to suffer pain and adversity. . . . There I go: having resolved never to write another word, I've already filled a page with the shadow of the shadow of a subject.

In fact, if it really was a tear it was so fleeting that by the time I was aware of it it no longer existed. All is transient in this world. If my eyes were not so bad I'd set about composing another Ecclesiastes, a modern version, even though after that book nothing can be considered modern. He said that there was nothing new under the sun, and if there wasn't then, there wasn't before and never will be again. Everything is contradictory as well as being confused.

27 August

The Aguiars' joy is apparent to all. Both husband and wife think up all manner of ways of passing the time with their two adopted children and with a few friends, among whom it seems I am included. They dine together, go for walks together, and if they do not organize balls it is because they themselves do not like them, though I am sure that if Fidelia and Tristão wanted they would arrange them. The truth is, however, that their two guests have not yet reached that stage, especially not Fidelia, who is content to smile and chat; she does not go to theatres or any public events.

Their walks are circumscribed as regards time and place. Sometimes the women go alone, sometimes the men go too, occasionally changing partners, Aguiar giving his arm to Fidelia and Dona Carmo accepting Tristão's. That's how they were the other day when I met them in Rua Ipiranga at five o'clock in the afternoon. The old couple seemed to show a certain pride in their own happiness. Dona Carmo's eyes and wide smile that revealed the shining tips of her teeth spoke eloquently of her joy in the son that was not hers, of the son who had died and risen again, while the lad himself showed pleasure in his attentions to her. Nor was the old man backward in revealing his delight. Fidelia, however, displayed no emotion; true, she smiled, but not often, and she did so with her head bowed. I was on the other side of the road, and they walked by without noticing me.

How I still love music! Last night there was a group of us at the Aguiars' house.... Thirteen! Only now, counting those present from memory, did I realize that we were thirteen. No one noticed the number either in the living room or at the tea table. We talked of one thing and another until finally Tristão, at his godmother's request, played some Mozart on the piano.

This happened because we had been discussing music, a subject which Fidelia took up with the new arrival with such enthusiam and good taste that at the end he asked her to play something too. She modestly declined, but Tristão insisted, and when his request was seconded by Dona Carmo and then by her husband, she gave way and played a short piece, a reminiscence by Schumann. We were all delighted. Tristão played a second time and they each seemed to appreciate the other's ability. I left the house enchanted with both of them. The music accompanied me, not allowing me to fall asleep. I arrived home early, eleven o'clock, but not until one did sleep finally come. All the time in the street, in the house and in bed I was hearing over and over again themes I had heard throughout my life.

I have always had an inclination for music, and if it weren't for fear of sounding poetical or, who knows, pathetic, I should say that it is one of the things I most regret. If I had learned music, perhaps today I might be able to play or compose. I decided not to because of the diplomatic service, and that was a mistake. The diplomacy I exercised in my life was more decorative than anything else. I made no commercial treaties or boundary agreements, nor did I help form any wartime alliances. I could have found time for the melodies of the drawing room or the study. Now I am dependent on what others play.

Two or three months ago I heard Fidelia say that she would never play again, having given up music a long time ago. At that time I replied that one day she would play again to herself, just to remember, and the remembrance would bring back the habit once more. Yesterday it only needed the Aguiars' insistence to arouse a disposition already half prepared, and Tristão's example provided the finishing touch. I repeat that I left the house enchanted with both of them.

Who knows if at this moment (half-past ten in the morning) she might not be at home, seated before the open piano, and astonishing her family and neighbours by striking up something she hasn't played for ages?

'It's not possible!'

'Dona Fidelia!'

'Noronha's widow!'

'It must be a friend of hers.'

And her fingers will play on, talking, thinking, living those notes that are there, stored away in the human memory. Probably she will play as she did yesterday, by heart, without music, the melody just flowing from her finger tips.

6 p.m.

Before going in to dinner I write to confirm my morning suppositions. Fidelia did in fact awaken the echoes in the house and the street. Judge Campos told me about it just now, the only difference being that it wasn't at half-past ten but at seven o'clock. Campos was still in bed when he heard the first notes of a well-known piece, Italian it seems. He couldn't believe it was her, but it couldn't be anyone else. He called a servant, who said yes, it was her. She played for some time. When he entered the drawing room she had finished but was still seated at the piano studying a score.

'What's the matter?' he asked.

'Did you hear me playing?' she asked, spinning round on the stool.

'Yes.'

'I think I've got rather out of practice, my fingers are a little stiff; I felt the same thing yesterday. I didn't forget the music though.'

'Is this a resurrection or something?'

'To do with the dead,' she replied with an attempt at a smile.

Considering he has no great love of music the Judge seems quite happy with that resurrection as he calls it. As he said, it is a question of living with more noise or less. He told me that he is often distressed by his niece's grief and, not taking her to balls or theatres, he would be happy to see her playing at home, and even singing if she wanted. Fidelia sings too, and she does so very well for she has a beautiful voice. But until now she has wanted neither one thing nor the other.

It is not as though she doesn't fill the house herself, even without music. But music was one of her former pastimes, one which she gave up on becoming a widow.

I wanted to point out to the Judge that the habit of playing music is quite in keeping with her condition since art itself is a form of language, but the idea slipped from my mind. It might have been too poetical for a judge, not to mention being indiscreet too. I simply accepted his invitation to go to his house to hear her today, tomorrow, the day after or whenever I wanted.

'One evening soon,' I said.

Meanwhile I'll go and have dinner. I don't think I'll go out again today, but what am I going to do about these wretched eyes of mine? If I read they get worse. Ah, if I only knew how to play! I'd take my violin, shut the doors tight so as not to disturb the neighbours, and fiddle away to my heart's content. I'll maybe go for a walk after all. . . .

2 September

The anniversary of the Battle of Sedan. I may go to the Judge's house to ask Fidelia to play us some Wagner in commemoration of the Prussian victory.

3 September

Neither Wagner nor anyone else. Tristão was there and played us a passage from *Tannhäuser*, but Fidelia refused my request. Imagining that this was due to grief at the memory of the French defeat, I asked her for something by any French composer, ancient or modern, since art, I said, with some affectation, makes us all citizens of a loftier state. She smiled but did not play, saying she had a slight headache. Aguiar and Carmo, who were there too, did not second my request, as if 'their friend's headache hurt them' – another preciosity of style, this one adapted from Sévigné. Watch that tongue of yours, old diplomat.

The real reason for her refusal may not be a headache, nor any other ache. It seems to me that Fidelia takes after me somewhat, and would play to herself if she were alone. That night at the Aguiars' she let herself be persuaded and played for the twelve people there, taken by surprise and by the awakening of her former enthusiasm. Now she shakes her head and does not want to entertain the others. She will play for her uncle in the morning, and to herself during court hours. At the most she will satisfy the Aguiars occasionally. Proof that she had no headache was that she listened to Tristão with evident pleasure and applauded him smiling warmly. I am not saying that music has not the power to make us forget physical pain, but I suspect that tonight this was not the case. . . .

The two talked about Wagner and other composers, what they said being interesting and probably correct. I too put in a few words, then gave my attention to what Aguiar was telling me about Tristão.

'It seems he also came to wind up some business of his father's. He told me himself this morning. I hope to God he doesn't get it finished too quickly.'

'God also likes chicanery, who knows.'

'There's nothing for the courts, but if something has to be decided there he'll probably leave a power of attorney. Did you know that he's going into parliament?'

'Yes, he told me that he had agreed with some of the Lisbon party leaders to be elected deputy.'

'Carmo, who was hoping to keep him here for a year or more, was very disappointed and upset, and I with her. We share our troubles, by which I mean that we add them together so that each gets double.'

I liked that expression of Aguiar's and learned it by heart so as not to forget it and to note it down here. The bank manager has not lost the vice of poetry. He's a good man. I think I've written that before, but even so I'll say it again. I lose nothing by repeating it.

We were talking in a corner of the room, and Campos and Tristão joined us, leaving the two ladies chatting together. I watched them from the distance, moved by their natural, unaffected charm. Seeing the white head of the one set against the black hair of the other, the smiles and whispers they exchanged and their eyes full of tenderness and love, all this made me ask myself why they were not really mother and daughter. One would be married to some deserving young man, the other married or widowed, it did not matter, for the eternal daughter would console her for the husband she had lost. All young daughters are eternal to the ageing mother. But once again I felt that they seemed more like sisters, such was Dona Carmo's knack of appearing young when with young people. I have no idea what they were talking about, nor is it worth while conjecturing, it would add nothing of interest. Once, when Fidelia was having difficulty arranging her brooch Dona Carmo's fingers took over and set it to rights.

4 September

Re-reading what I wrote yesterday a thought came to me which I will write down now in order to remember it later. Who knows if Dona Carmo's affection, dedicated and well-intentioned as it is, will not in the long run be injurious to the lovely Fidelia? Although a widow, her future is marriage: she is of an age to marry, and quite likely someone will come along who will really want her for his wife. I don't mean myself, for heaven's sake; I was merely indulging in a sexagenarian's pipe dreams; I mean a real person who could and would love her as she deserves. Left to herself she would accept him, and together they would make their way to the altar; but as the friend of Dona Carmo, in her care, the suitor will go unregarded and her future be thrown away. Instead of being the mother of a family she will remain a lonely widow, for the old friend will die one day, as will the girl herself . . . after many days.

No matter what is said to the contrary, this is the truth. I'm not claiming that things will work out exactly like that, and that the three of them – four, if we count Aguiar, five and six if we include the uncle and cousin – might not, with the eventual suitor, make up a happy, united family; but the truth remains. Affection, habit, growing influence, and lastly time, the accomplice in so much injustice, will rob the beautiful widow of any lover fate or society might throw in her path. And so she will reach thirty, then thirty-five, then forty. When Senhora Aguiar dies, not content with mourning her, she will cling to her memory and her grief will increase with the passing years. The suitor will have disappeared or found his happiness elsewhere.

Re-reading today's notes also, I feared that (particularly at the end) I might have added too romantic or poetic a touch. But that is not so; it is all prose, like reality itself. I forgot to mention a further argument in favour of the girl's continuing widowhood, the memory of her husband. In five years' time she will have her father's remains brought to her husband's grave, and will join the two together on earth just as they have already been joined together in eternity. Here and in the hereafter politics means no more than living together, one with the other, exactly as they were, and for all eternity.

8 September

The Aguiars' two adopted children are not jealous of each other and neither feels slighted by the affection the other receives from the old couple. On the contrary, they seem to feel that what each receives increases the share of both. An example of true friendship: there are cases where real children do not display the same goodwill.

I mentioned this to my sister Rita, and she agrees with me. She also added an observation even shrewder than mine, and I have no scruples in recording it here beside my own, the more so since I replied with another no less shrewd. A pretty compliment to both of us! Since there are always people ready to run us down I'll let that stand as it is in compensation. It costs nothing to sing one's own praises. This is what my sister said: 'Such feelings don't cost Tristão very much seeing that he is here for such a short time.'

To which I replied: 'They don't cost Fidelia much either knowing that he'll be leaving before long.'

Looking now at the written words I have my doubts about Rita's and my shrewdness. No matter how short the lad's visit he would like to see himself the exclusive object of their affection, as also would she. Once again I came to the conclusion that it is the nature of their filial affection that makes them so open-hearted and generous. I repeat what I said above – there are cases where the real children do not live in such harmony.

Rita gave me more news of the Aguiars' house, where I haven't set foot for over a week I think. It served to confirm how well the old folk and the young get on. The four of them spend the days talking together, and yesterday Fidelia played the piano, just a little it's true, but she did play. And apparently once they played cards.

'Fidelia,' Rita went on, 'who has never done any needlework since she left school, has now begun to imitate her friend, and yesterday they were working away together. When I arrived there at two o'clock I found them sitting busy with their needles, and you can't imagine how pleased they were to see me. Dona Carmo was quite proud of herself, or so it seemed. They were making a pair of children's shoes. Fidelia's work was not so perfect as the old lady's, nor so advanced, and I think Dona Carmo could have worked quicker but, not wanting to leave the girl too far behind, she kept her fingers in check. I was going to laugh and ask which one of them the shoes were for, but I had no chance. Fidelia told me they were for the baby of one of Dona Carmo's maids, who had gone to her husband's house to give birth. Dona Carmo was beginning her crochet when Fidelia arrived and wanted to help her. She agreed so that the work would not be entirely that of an old woman.

I won't include the rest of what Rita had to say so as not to waste time and paper, but it was interesting. I'll just add this, that she dined there, Fidelia too, at Dona Carmo's invitation. Aguiar and Tristão had gone for a walk after lunch, but returned early, at four o'clock. They didn't see yesterday's military parade, just a battalion marching past, which failed to impress Tristão. All battalions look alike, he said. But he admitted that the national anthem awoke in him memories of his childhood and youth, and that led to the conversation about music which brought Fidelia to the piano. She only played for four or five minutes, and it was at Tristão's request, for he suggested a composer. Rita doesn't remember which composer it was but she liked the music. They also talked about Europe, and the two seemed to have many ideas in common.

I heard all this in Andaraí, where I went today to have dinner with Rita. I suggested that she come with me to Flamengo, but she refused, saying that she was tired and wanted to go to bed. I came back alone and went to the Aguiars', where the four of them and the Judge were discussing religious festivals on account of the saint's day today. Once again the two gave their impressions of Europe, and they do really have much in common. Mine, whenever they were asked for, were limited to a nodded agreement, which is useful when you find the subject boring or disagreeable, as I did.

I stayed on with the Aguiars for another quarter of an hour after the uncle and niece had left. The rest tomorrow; I need some sleep too.

9 September

The rest is the news of the return of Osorio, the lawyer of the Do Sul Bank who went to Recife some time ago where his father was ill and later died.

'He came back very sad, and the mourning makes him look even more so,' said Aguiar.

'Is it just on account of his father's death?' I asked.

'What else could it be?'

'Didn't they tell me, or did I guess that he was half in love with Dona Fidelia?'

'Yes, he was, and perhaps more than half,' explained Aguiar. 'But he's getting over it.'

'In any case, didn't he propose?'

'It's possible he made some kind of gesture, which she tacitly refused. A pity, as they are well suited.'

Aguiar praised the lad's professional qualities, his upbringing and virtues, and I dutifully believed it all; in any case I had no reason to doubt him. Dona Carmo confirmed what her husband had said, but without declaring it was a pity they had not married. She remained silent on this point, showing more discretion than her husband. Possibly in him it was the bank manager speaking. All this time Tristão was browsing through a book of engravings.

I say they were engravings because I went up to him to say goodbye, and he rose to his feet politely, but from a distance I thought it was a photograph album. It wasn't: the photograph album was next to it, and open at the page which has two photographs of Dona Carmo and her husband. Tristão left the book of engravings open too and accompanied Aguiar and me to the door, where I took my leave.

9 September, afternoon

It seems that the Aguiars are instilling in me a taste for children, or regrets for them, which is a more amusing way of putting it. Just now in Rua Gloria I came across seven children, boys and girls of different ages, walking in line, hand in hand. Their youth, their laughter and their agility attracted my attention, and I stopped on the pavement to watch them. Their movements were so graceful and they all seemed so friendly that I began to laugh out of sheer pleasure. My account would end here, if I ever wrote it, were it not for the expression used by one of them, a little girl, who saw me standing there laughing, and said to her companions, 'Look at that lad who's laughing at us.'

Her words revealed to me how children see us. Me, with my white moustache and grey hair, they called 'lad'. They probably use the term according to the height of the person without bothering to inquire his age.

I left the children at their play and walked on, making this reflection to myself. They went skipping away, stopping occasionally, jumping to the right, then to the left, breaking the line and then reforming again. I don't know where they went off to, but I know that after ten minutes not one was left in sight. But then came more children, singly or in pairs, some carrying heavy bundles or baskets on their heads or shoulders – already working at an age when those others were still at play. It might be said that never having had to carry anything in my childhood is the reason for my appearing a 'lad' to the first group of children. But no, it wasn't that. Age sees things as they are; children's eyes do not discriminate. If I laughed now these others would think 'that lad was laughing at them'. But I was serious, pensive, perhaps feeling in my own bones the weariness of those children who, not realizing that my white hair ought to have seemed to them black, went on their way, and so did I.

On reaching the front door of my house I met my man José, who said he was waiting for me.

'What for?'

'No reason – I just came to wait for you.'

It was a lie; he came to stretch his legs or else to watch the neighbours' maids as they passed by, like him in need of some distraction. But since he is clever, resourceful, serious, devoted to his duty, possessed of all talents and virtues, he preferred to lie nobly than to admit the truth. I nobly forgave him and went for a nap before dinner.

It was a short nap, just twenty minutes, barely sufficient to dream that all the children in the world, with or without burdens on their heads, had formed a huge circle around me and were dancing so merrily that I was almost bursting with laughter. All were saying, '. . . that lad who laughs so much.' I woke up feeling hungry, washed and dressed and came to write this down. Now I'll have dinner, and probably go to Flamengo.

9 September, at night

I went to Flamengo. Fidelia wasn't there, but Osorio was, though I didn't find him as gloomy as Aguiar had said, nor cheerful either; he spoke little. Tristão, who had been introduced to him today, spoke more than him and even he didn't say much. A dull night. I came home early and I'm off to bed.

12 September

I arrived in the city at two o'clock today, and just as I was getting out of the tram the beautiful Fidelia, as graceful and austere as ever, came running to catch it. She had been shopping of course. We greeted each other and I gave her my hand to help her up. She asked after my sister, I after her uncle, and both about each other, and we still had time to exchange the following half-dozen words.

'Coming to town so late?' she asked.

'The indolence proper to retirement did not allow me to leave earlier,' I said with a laugh as I walked away.

The tram left. At the corner was none other than Dr Osorio, bereft of his eyes because she had carried them off with her on the tram. That I assumed to be the explanation for his blindness when I passed by without him seeing me. My goodness, what style!

A thought came to me: had they been together in the street, or in the shop she visited, or in the bank, or in hell (which also has its lovers, no doubt the sinful ones, *del mal perverso*)? I decided not, imagining that if by chance he greeted her in the street he would not dare to stop and speak, but would watch her from a distance until he saw her get into the tram and depart.

Another thing occurred to me, which was that his former, rejected passion had either never died, or had revived at the renewed sight of her person. It wasn't because she is now a wealthy woman; before she had been the sole heir and had had independent means. No, he's a fine lad, and Aguiar himself says they are well suited.

I was walking towards the Polytechnic, pondering all these things, when I saw him pass by, head bowed, but whether in sorrow or joy I don't know as I couldn't see his face. But I think it is sorrow that bows our head; in joy our eyes gaze round about to right and left, and even up to the heavens. But the truth of the matter is that that lawyer, at two o'clock in the afternoon, was out looking at girls instead of being in court. He's either a bad lawyer or a successful lover.

14 September

He's neither one thing nor the other. I am referring to what I wrote the day before yesterday about Osorio, who is neither a successful lover, according to what Aguiar told me today, nor a bad lawyer, from what I read in the papers. I read that he won a lawsuit for the Do Sul Bank and Aguiar could not speak well enough of his handling of the case, both before he left and after his return. There's a man for you who can unite zeal with sorrow, and this might well be symbolic, his being the zeal and Fidelia's the sorrow. Maybe they'll end up marrying. But even after her refusal? Everything is possible under the sun – and it may well be the same above it. Only God knows.

I've just come from the Aguiars' and I don't want to go to bed before writing down what happened there. I arrived early; the old couple were on their own and greeted me warmly.

'Come in old fellow,' he said. 'Come and make a third with two old folks who have been left abandoned here.'

These words, which might have been taken for a complaint, were spoken with a laugh, and I saw from his tone that he was in a good mood. They were spoken near the door, where he had come to greet me, leaving Dona Carmo in one of the two rocking chairs placed side by side like a two-way chair, where they used to spend their solitary hours. I answered that I had brought my old age to add to theirs and so form a single green youth the like of which is no longer seen in this world. They made some amusing remarks on this old, worn-out theme, and so the first few minutes passed.

'You might not have found us here if I didn't have a bad knee,' said Dona Carmo.

'A bad knee?'

'Yes, this one hurts me a little and makes it difficult to walk. Tristão went on his own to the Judge's, where he's entertaining some friends from the court. Aguiar wanted to go too, but Tristão said it would be better if he stayed. He promised to make our excuses and went on his own.'

'He wanted me to stay and keep Carmo company,' explained Aguiar. 'If I had insisted he would probably have stayed himself so as not to leave her on her own.'

Dona Carmo seemed to give her assent with her eyes.

Only with her eyes. Then out loud she said that he probably went in the hope of meeting some girls there. It was likely that the old friends would take their daughters.

'Then it's a party of some kind?' I asked.

'No, Counsellor,' said Aguiar. 'It's just three or four friends who agreed among themselves to go there today, and warned the Judge in advance. That's what Fidelia told us yesterday here at home.'

Dona Carmo took up what she had been saying before: 'Some of them will take their daughters, and it's only natural for a young man to want to meet some young girls. Tristão finds his countrywomen very charming, as he has said more than once. And if there aren't any there I expect he'll cut his visit short and come home. He seems closer to us every day.'

I knew as much and nodded my agreement. Aguiar said the same thing. What he didn't mention, and what I had not expected, was the note of sadness that was brought into the conversation by his wife. This I tried to dispel as far as I could.

'The days are passing quickly,' she said, 'and the last ones will pass even more quickly. Soon our Tristão will be returning to Lisbon and will never come back, or if he does it will be just to visit our graves.'

'Come now, Dona Carmo, you mustn't give way to such gloomy thoughts.'

'Carmo's right,' put in her husband. 'Time will rush by until he leaves, nor will it stand still awaiting our bidding so that we may live on for ever.'

'The time comes for all of us,' I said. 'Death is another of those judges with many friends who go to spend the evening with him, and those who have daughters take their daughters. That's the truth, but it's best not to think of it.'

'It's not that so much,' said Dona Carmo. 'I'm thinking of our Tristão, who'll soon be leaving us.'

I gave a smile and said, '*He* will leave, but *she* will be staying.'

I emphasized the pronouns but it was hardly necessary; Carmo understood me immediately. The broad smile that spread over her face showed that she caught the allusion to the beautiful Fidelia. This was her great comfort. Nevertheless, comfort comes to solace pain, and the pain of losing one was no less than the pleasure of keeping the other. I saw both these expressions on the old lady's face, joined together in one to form a kind of half-sadness. Aguiar too must have felt the same as his wife, but being a bank manager had accustomed him to the necessity of dissimulation. Perhaps they had not yet spoken among themselves about Tristão's return. Felicity rhymes with eternity, and they were happy.

They were happy, and it was the husband who first took up enumerating Tristão's latest virtues. His wife joined in on the same theme and I had to listen to them with my usual dispassion, which though one of *my* virtues is not one of the latest. I have had it ever since school, if not from the cradle. My mother used to say that I rarely cried for my bottle, just pulled a face and gave a supplicating look. At school I quarrelled with no one; I listened to the teacher and I listened to my companions, and if these became violent in their quarrels I, in my wisdom, saw both sides of the question. They ended up punching each other but treating me with respect.

I have no wish to sing my own praises. . . . Where was I? Ah yes, at the point where the old couple were listing the young fellow's virtues. They weren't lying; at most they may have exaggerated one or two, but on the whole they were correct. He is good, kind hearted, attentive, honest, good natured, peace loving, well mannered and capable of sacrificing his own interests should it be necessary. On his arrival they found nothing bad, nothing to object to; now, however, his former qualities have all improved and new ones appeared. Even if I disagreed with them I would not say so in order not to distress them; but what did I know that might contradict my friends' opinion? Nothing, so I merely agreed with them both.

Dona Carmo, perhaps realizing that the subject might be boring to strangers, changed the course of the conversation. Not entirely, it is true, for she mentioned Judge Campos's house and what might be going on there. I (cunningly I admit), wanting to know the state of Osorio's sentiments, asked if he was there too since he also is connected with the court. Aguiar was quick to answer that he probably was; it depended. We spoke of this a little, and the lawyer's virtues were duly praised, though these were neither so numerous nor so outstanding as those of Tristão. They both spoke warmly of him, Aguiar more so than

Dona Carmo, though in matters more properly related to the bank and the courts.

'But isn't there anything left of the old spark in him?' I asked.

'Could be,' said Aguiar. 'And it would be a further reason for him staying away.'

I did not mention what I had seen in the street, and in any case his own conclusion was not wrong. Dona Carmo did not speak, but she was listening attentively. I have nowhere else met anyone with a greater sense of discretion than she has. She did not want to enter into the subject, and her husband soon afterwards dropped it. I did not press the matter.

Such is the fate of unfortunate lovers: even their friends, as Aguiar seems to be of Osorio, hasten to change the subject. They are left to themselves. We turned to discussing society news and the latest novels from Paris. On this score Dona Carmo knows more than I do, and much more than her husband, who knows nothing at all, though he takes part in the conversation as if he did. He buys books for her to read, and she summarizes them for him to listen to. As he has a good memory he is able to refer to the texts, but with the difference that since his wife's knowledge is first hand her impressions are livelier and more interesting. I heard her make some shrewd comments on several contemporary writers. Of course, if her husband were also a writer she would find him the best of all, for she is deeply in love with him, as much as or more so than on the day she married him. That was the impression I gained today.

In order to please them – and myself too, since I enjoy giving them pleasure – I returned to the principal subject for both of them, which was not just Fidelia, or just Tristão, but the two of them together.

'Tell me, if they were really brother and sister, and your children, wouldn't it be better than just being friends, strangers to each other?'

This was the first time I had ever asked them anything like that, and their interest was such that they seized upon the theme to make the most fascinating observations. I won't write them now as it is late, but I have them stored in my memory. I will merely say that when I left, in spite of her bad knee and all my remonstrances, Dona Carmo accompanied us to the door. Aguiar went with me to the garden gate while she said goodbye once again from the window.

'Goodnight, and mind the damp air,' I called back.

'Goodnight.'

Dona Carmo went in and Aguiar and I shook hands. On going out I remembered I wanted to speak about the dog buried there. I was not able to bring the subject up immediately, managing it only after three or four attempts, rapid ones, not taking over a minute, if that. He heard me both astonished and embarrassed.

'Who told you that?'

'Dr Tristão.'

I didn't want to mention Campos, who had also told me about the animal. Aguiar muttered something, then spoke about it without saying much. He told me how fond they had been of the dog and his wife's sufferings when it fell ill and died. He didn't mention his own, though he suffered too. He glanced down beside the wall, then said, 'No doubt Tristão had a good laugh at our fondness for a dog.'

'On the contrary, he was warm in his praise. He has a good heart, that lad.'

'Very good.'

Though I am not given to melancholy and do not hold with the banking profession indulging in griefs of that nature, we parted on the friendliest of terms. I walked home along Rua da Princesa thinking of them both, paying no heed to a dog which, on hearing my footsteps, started barking from inside a garden. There is never any lack of dogs at our heels, some ugly, some pretty and all of them a nuisance. As I neared Rua Catete the barking began to die away, and it seemed to be sending me this message: 'My friend, you needn't wonder why I am addressing you like this; to bark and to die is a dog's function, and the Aguiars' dog too used to bark in times past. Now it forgets, which also is a function of the dead.'

I considered this observation so subtle and so profound that I preferred to attribute it to some dog barking inside my own brain. When I was a young man, travelling in Europe, I heard a certain singer referred to as an elephant who had swallowed a nightingale. I think they were referring to Alboni, who had an enormous body but an exquisite voice. So I may well have swallowed a philosophical dog, making the merit of this discourse all his. Who knows what my cook may have served me on some past occasion. And it was nothing new for me to compare the voices of the living with those of the dead.

20 September

That day, the 18th of September (the day before yesterday) will always remain more clearly and firmly fixed in my memory than any other on account of the evening we three old people spent together. Maybe I haven't written everything, and not all that well, but just re-reading it yesterday brought back vivid, interesting recollections of the old lady, the old man, the memory of their two adopted children. . . . I continue to call them that for lack of a better name. And especially that state of in-between or clouded happiness of people who are about to lose one of their two heaven-sent gifts, more observable in Dona Carmo than in Aguiar. . . .

21 September

When I left the house this morning I saw Miranda's sister, Dona Cesaria, passing by on the opposite side of the street. She looked so happy that it seemed she was speaking ill of me. But she wasn't speaking, she was alone – or speaking of me to herself. But that wouldn't give her so much pleasure. We waved to each other and went on our way.

22 September

. . . charming Fidelia! I don't write this out of desire for her, but because that is exactly what she is: charming. For didn't this heavenly creature, on seeing me this morning, come and thank me for keeping her friends company in Flamengo on the evening of the 18th?

'I deserve no thanks for that. I went there, found them alone and spent the evening with them.'

'That's what I meant. Dona Carmo told me that it only needed Dr Tristão and myself to make it a full evening, and even so you managed to make them forget us.'

I gave an incredulous smile, and explained the matter, saying that if I caused them to be forgotten it was because they themselves were the subject of the conversation.

'She didn't tell me that,' said Fidelia, in astonishment.

'She won't do so, and you had better not ask. The best thing is just to believe that I, with my white hair, helped them to pass the time. You have no idea the things that are said when three old people get together, if at any time in their lives they have thought or felt anything.'

'I know, I know. I've seen you together, and heard you too.'

'But on those occasions you were there to add a touch of youth and gaiety to the conversation.'

Although intended as a compliment, this was true. Fidelia smiled her thanks and said goodbye. I – and I say this before God and the Devil, if the latter gentleman is also interested in this journal of mine – I decided to follow her. It was not curiosity, much less any other thing, simply aesthetic appreciation. She has a graceful walk; she was what I said above, charming. She did not appear aware of this fact, though she must have been. I have never yet met a charming woman who was not. The mere supposition of being so persuades her that she is.

Her cab was waiting in São Francisco Square, near the church. We were walking down Rua do Ouvidor about ten steps apart or a little more. I halted at the corner and watched her walk on, stop, speak to the cabby and enter the cab, which then set off down a side street in the direction, naturally, of the Judge's house in Botafogo. When I was about to turn back I met young Tristão, who was still gazing at the cab in the middle of the square as if he had seen her get in. He was making for Rua do Ouvidor, and when he noticed me too I stopped to wait for him. He turned his dazzled eyes on me.

'A wonderful talent!'

Realizing he was referring to her musical talent, I was so astonished that I nearly forgot to agree with him. I did so finally with a word and a gesture, but without understanding anything. Like him I am fond of music, and regret not being able to play to beguile my loneliness, but if I were him, and in spite of all the Schumanns and the like, on seeing her stop in São Francisco Square and get into a cab I would not make the same observation but another; this would reveal equal aesthetic appreciation, but it would be visual, not auditive. I did not understand at first.

Later, when we parted on the corner of Rua da Quitanda, I began to wonder whether, on meeting me, he had spoken those words with the object of showing that what he most admires about her is her musical talent. It could be so; he has a good deal of modesty and not a little dissimulation. Not wishing to appear an admirer of a shapely foot, he referred rather to her nimble fingers. But it all added up to the same person.

30 September

If I were writing a novel I would omit the pages referring to the 12th and 22nd of this month. In a novel such coincidences would not be allowed. On both those days – which I would then call chapters – I met Fidelia in the street, we chatted together, I watched her get into a tram or a cab and depart, and then I met two young fellows who seemed to be admiring her. I'd leave out those two chapters or else re-write them differently, in which case I would be departing from the exact truth, which here appears to me more important than in a work of the imagination.

Some pages ago I spoke of coincidences that occur in life, mentioning the cases of Osorio and Fidelia, both of whose parents fell ill far from here, obliging both young people to leave and visit them. All this has no place in works of the imagination, which call for more variety and contradictions. But life is like that, a repetition of the same actions and behaviour, such as in receptions, visits, meals and other social activities. In our working lives the same thing applies. No matter how much chance may interfere, events frequently turn out alike both in their circumstances and their timing. It's like that in history and in everything else.

I make this justification to myself in order to mention that I have a bad knee just like Dona Carmo. Another coincidence. . . . There are, however, two differences. The first is that hers is purely a case of rheumatism, openly admitted. Mine is too, though my man José calls it neuralgia, either to sound more elegant or less painful. The second difference. . . .

The second difference – ah, for God's sake! The second difference is that although her knee may be very painful, Dona Carmo has her husband and her two adopted children. I have my wife under the ground in Vienna, while none of my children ever emerged from non-existence. I am alone, completely alone. Noises from the street – coaches, animals, people, bells and whistles – nothing of this has any significance for me. At most the clock on the wall chiming the hours seems to have something to say, but it speaks little and in a dull, funereal voice. Re-reading these last few lines I feel like a gravedigger.

My sister Rita hasn't been to see me because she doesn't know; probably she hasn't been outdoors, though I know she is well. The trouble started a week ago. I sleep well at night, but walking is painful. Tomorrow, if I'm no worse, I'll go out.

2 October

I'm better, but it rained and I didn't go out.

3 October

'It was a duel between myself and old age that put this bullet in my knee. It's a rheumatic pain. I assume you have come to have dinner with me?'

Campos replied that he hadn't; hearing that I was ill he had come to find out what was the matter. Dona Carmo's knee is also better, he said. She is able to get around, but not far, only from Flamengo to Russel beach.

'Always with her young friend, I expect?'

'Not always. Tristão goes with her in the mornings. Fidelia asks to be remembered to you, and perhaps Aguiar will come round later today. Like me they only heard about you yesterday evening.'

Shortly afterwards Campos told me that his niece wanted to spend some time at the fazenda. 'In spite of the love they have, or claim to have for her, the freed slaves are beginning to leave their work, and she wants to find out what the situation is before selling up.'

98

I didn't quite understand, but did not like to ask for further explanation. Campos said that he too doesn't understand his niece's intentions, adding that she is anxious to leave right away. It was Dona Carmo's illness that persuaded her to accept her uncle's suggestion and postpone the trip until the holidays.

'We'll go there in the holidays,' he concluded. 'If the administrator hasn't been able to stop the men from leaving up till now, he won't be able to by then. Fidelia thinks that her presence alone will stop them leaving.'

'In that case, the sooner she goes. . . .' I observed, with an attempt at a smile.

'That is what she said. But I don't think it makes all that much difference, and since I have to go with her, I prefer December to October. It seems to me that it is not so much the loss of the freed slaves that worries her as something else. . . .'

He left the sentence unfinished, got up to adjust a loop of the curtain and returned, scratching his chin and gazing at the ceiling. He sat down and crossed his legs. To avoid asking questions I seized on his gesture and commented that for me to do with my legs what he had done with his would not be easy. But I might have been talking to the curtain, the loop or the mat on the floor. Campos made no reply, and probably never heard me. He got up saying that he was glad to see me better, and said goodbye. I insisted that he stay to dinner.

'I can't, I have people coming. Tristão's dining with me.'

To prove I was on the mend I went as far as the landing with him, stepping out firmly. I thanked him for his visit and returned to the room visualizing Fidelia on her way to the fazenda. But what can it possibly be that takes her out to the fazenda with its half-dozen freed slaves, that is if she finds any at all? A little later came another visitor, Aguiar, bringing best wishes from his wife. He was delighted to see me on my feet in the middle of the drawing room.

'You needn't have come,' I said. 'It was nothing, really. I'm almost better, and today if the rain stops, as it seems likely to, I'll go home with you after dinner. Will you have dinner with me?'

'I can't, I have people coming. One of them would be no problem: that's Fidelia, who's dining with us. She's like one of

99

the family. But there's also a colleague from the bank coming.'

'Well, I'll call by for tea.'

'Come if you want to, but I wouldn't advise it. Even if it doesn't rain it is still damp, and for rheumatism. . .'

'But Dona Carmo has been out, I believe.'

'Yes, and she's better too. In spite of that she didn't go out today because of the weather. Come if you wish, but in your place I wouldn't leave the house.'

Aguiar left without saying any more. I had the impression (or was it an illusion?) that there was something more that he wanted to add but never got round to. I have no idea what it could be. If I wasn't too scared of the damp I'd go round and see them tonight, but the damp is certain, and rain too, I think. I'll stay at home. If any chess player calls I'll play chess; if just a card player, cards. And if no one comes I'll compose some poetry in my head.

6 October

Rita, Rita, sister dear,
That was your last visit here,

and the rest will have to be in prose because my muse is now exhausted. That's what I composed not that evening of the 3rd, but today, the 6th, after taking my sister home to Andaraí. She came to see me this morning. Other friends and even casual visitors had called to see me, like that Dr Faria, who brought best wishes from his wife, and the broker, Miranda, who also brought his wife's. Tristão called the day before yesterday, and I ventured out that afternoon and yesterday morning, too. I'm well again, but even so I took her to task for her ingratitude. Rita admitted that for three weeks she had not left the house to find out if she still had a brother who remembered her.

'You had, and still have,' I replied. 'But a brother who has only now completely recovered.'

I told her of the pain and of being laid up. At first Rita didn't believe me and treated it as a joke, but finally she was convinced and more contrite. Naturally she gave me a lecture, but I explained that I was keeping her in reserve for my last, mortal illness. We chatted away agreeably, occasionally cheerfully. When I asked her if she had been to the Aguiars' or to Campos's, she said she hadn't, for had she been to either house she would have learned of my condition, and she had had no news of me.

'Then you don't know about the idea of going to the fazenda?' I asked.

'Whose idea?'

'Fidelia's.'

'To go to the fazenda?'

'Yes, to go to Santa-Pia to see how things are. It seems the freed slaves are abandoning the place. That's what her uncle told me.'

'I haven't heard anything about it. I haven't been outside the house for almost a month. But why doesn't her uncle go?'

'He is going, but with her. She wants his company, but apparently only his company, not his assistance. They're going in the holidays. I can't understand the necessity of her going too, when a man would be much better.'

Rita wanted to go and find out why from Fidelia herself. I pointed out that this might be indiscreet, showing undue curiosity on our part. Nevertheless, she went out and came back some time later. I confess one thing: as soon as I saw her go out I guessed she must have gone to find out from Fidelia or her friends the real reason for the journey, and I told her so at dinner. She looked serious and shook her head. Had she sworn the contrary it is likely I should have had my doubts, but she spoke quite naturally and told me of the visits she had made, one of which was to Dona Carmo.

'Carmo is as right as rain,' she said. 'She was as happy as could be, and greeted me with that special laugh of hers, so open-hearted and frank. . . . We spoke about Fidelia and we spoke about Tristão, she with all the tenderness and affection that you know already.'

'Doesn't she know about the trip to the fazenda?'

'Yes, she does, and it seems they are not going to wait for the holidays – they are going in a few days' time. She knows about the trip and the reason for it, and has given her approval, saying that the freed slaves have great respect for Fidelia. If she could she would go too, but Aguiar won't be left on his own and he can't leave the bank at this moment.'

'But he wouldn't be on his own: Tristão's there.'

'No he won't be, and for two reasons. The first is that neither Tristão nor anyone else can be a substitute for his dear Carmo. The trip she made to Nova Friburgo this year was bad enough. It wasn't she who told me, I found out for myself; it's obvious, everyone knows that Aguiar without Carmo is nothing. The second reason is that Tristão himself wants to go with Campos and Fidelia. He has never seen a fazenda and wants to do so before he returns to Lisbon.'

'And how has our friend taken this sudden departure of the two of them? Isn't she very upset?'

'I asked her that, and she said she hopes it will be for a few days; in any case, if the others delay Tristão will come back on his own. He wants to spend as much time with her and her husband as he can.'

My sister (it is clear) is anxious to find some serious fault in Aguiar's godson, and is annoyed that she can't find one, serious or otherwise. When she speaks well of him she admits she is only repeating what she has heard. My tendency is to think well rather than ill, as I believe I have already written somewhere in these pages, but whether well or ill I didn't say. I limited myself to condemning my miserable dinner, which was wretched, only the chicken being any good, and the fruit (although not the pears). Over coffee Rita told me some of the goings-on in Andaraí, where I took her about ten o'clock, and from where I returned to write this, finishing off as I began:

> Rita, Rita, sister dear,
> That was your last visit here.

10 October

Can anyone understand women? It was imperative to rush off to the fazenda at once. Campos arranges a few days' leave of absence, Tristão packs his case, and lo and behold! there is no longer any need to go. Campos and Tristão went off on their own. That's what the two of them (Carmo and Fidelia) told me this afternoon as I entered the garden in Flamengo. They were coming towards the gate.

'I didn't go,' said Fidelia, in confirmation of Dona Carmo's last words. 'One man is more than enough to settle any problems there. In any case matters are improving.'

'All the better for your friends,' I said.

Dona Carmo assented, not in words but with her eyes. They were going for a walk so, after Dona Carmo and I had exchanged reports on our rheumatism, I offered to accompany them. We were both better. The two ladies walked arm in arm with me beside them, between them and the sea, which is calm today. Our conversation was desultory because Fidelia kept her eyes fixed on the ground. Her companion spoke to me but from time to time glanced at her, as I did too. Fidelia hardly spoke, and only then looked up at her.

Our walk being a short one, I returned with them to the garden, where soon afterwards Aguiar arrived bringing three or four letters from Lisbon for Tristão. I recognized the writing on one of them; it was from his father, and it was so bulky there was probably another inside from his mother. He had thought of sending them on to Santa-Pia, but not knowing whether the lad was coming back tomorrow or the next day, or was intending to stay longer, he had not done so. If he was coming back soon he would wait; if he was staying longer he would send them on. He had decided to consult his wife.

Dona Carmo thought the best thing would be to write a note asking when he intended returning, to know whether or not to forward the correspondence. Fidelia said she knew nothing about her uncle's return, but thought it likely he would stay on a few days longer to make the final arrangements and prepare the papers necessary for the sale of the house and property. These were being sold through the Do Sul Bank, but neither she nor Aguiar knew anything definite.

When asked my opinion I said that once he knew of the large amount of correspondence awaiting him, and assuming some to be of a political nature, Tristão would either ask for it to be sent to him right away or else come to collect it in person. This second hypothesis appealed more to his godmother, who regarded it as certain. After all, what was to keep him there once he had seen the fazenda? And the fazenda naturally could be seen quickly as it had no personal memories for him or former habits to revive. That is what I said in so many words, and the old couple agreed with me. I asked Fidelia if she had no regrets for the house where she had been born and brought up, and she replied that she did, but no longer had any wish to live there.

'It needs a man to look after it now,' she concluded.

Dona Carmo heard these words with intense pleasure, and Aguiar would probably have felt the same, but he had gone into the street to speak to a neighbour and did not hear. When he came back he thought I was taking my leave of the ladies, but even so he invited me to stay to dinner. I declined and left them. As I was leaving I heard him say to them, 'I wonder what's in those letters.'

Walking home I was sorry I had not stayed for dinner. I might have heard the 'wonderful talent' that had prompted Tristão's exclamation. It would be no novelty for me, just another opportunity, though it seems she has taken to declining all requests to play the piano. True, the two may be taking her to Botafogo tonight, but on the other hand she might spend the night there with her 'adopted parents'.

12 October

Aguiar and Dona Carmo took their young friend to Botafogo yesterday and returned home early. That is what he told me today at the door of the bank, where he found me in conversation with Miranda. There is no news of Tristão, but Aguiar's note is already in the post and on its way to Santa-Pia.

May it fly on the wings of the post, I write here in my journal, heedless of the highflown image. I pay heed to it now, but I shall neither cross it out nor find a substitute. Wings of the post will do very well so long as they reach the fazenda safely and don't lose the note on the way. I suspect that I too am curious to know what is in those letters from Lisbon, but it's just curiosity, and incidentally it is not surprising that this time they are so numerous and so bulky as up to now they have had little to say. Be that as it may, the old couple are anxious to know whether they are ordering him home. They don't say so but one can tell. Miranda went on telling me how they had all missed me, his wife, his sister-in-law Cesaria and his brother-in-law Faria, all of which I listened to gratefully, promising to go and pay my respects one of these days. The broker is not a bad fellow after all, and has already been of service to me professionally on one occasion. He has a lively manner, though without being boisterous, and is fascinated by things quite destitute of any interest whatever.

13 October

Campos wrote to his niece giving an account of the state of the fazenda and telling of the excursions he had made round it with young Tristão. The latter is both curious and discreet in his observation of things and the questions he asks. He tells of the priest and the Justice of the Peace. Since the letter was written before Aguiar's note he does not refer to it, but says that Tristão won't stay long and is planning to return in a few days.

Dona Carmo is hoping that these days will be curtailed as soon as he receives her husband's note. She didn't say so when I was there yesterday evening, neither did anyone else tell me; it was what I was able to read in her face. The Judge's letter was shown to her by Fidelia herself, who went there yesterday and this time played the piano, I don't know if as well as Tristão, but certainly well. The two ought to play together. There were just five of us there; Fidelia's student cousin brought her and then escorted her back to Botafogo at ten o'clock.

17 October

Tristão has arrived. I have no idea what he has read in his letters from Lisbon as I haven't met any of the people who might know. I'll go to Flamengo at some point, maybe tomorrow.

Today being my birthday I shall not leave the house. Today makes me sixty. . . . Don't write the whole figure, dear old chap; it is enough that your heart should know, and that Time goes on making his entries in his profit and loss account. Don't write everything, dear friend.

I won't leave the house. If Rita comes for dinner like she did last year I'll take her home to Andaraí at night. If she doesn't come, then I'll just stay on my own.

I'll pass the time looking through some old papers that my man José found in an old suitcase and has just brought to me. He had that pleased expression of one who has unexpectedly rendered a good service. He was wide-eyed and beaming, almost overjoyed at the thought of having discovered papers that might well be important.

'I expect you've been looking for them for ages.'

They were letters, jottings, minutes, accounts, a hellish jumble of relics that would have been better off left unfound. What did I lose without them? I never suspected their existence and would never miss them. And now I have to make a choice between two alternatives, either to read them first or burn them right away. I am inclined to the second. José stood there in front of me with the same happy expression brought about by his discovery. Naturally he is thanking his lucky stars that led him to the find, assured that this will be a further bond between us. Perhaps what led him to the suitcase was the hope of finding some mislaid valuable, a jewel for instance, or if not that a shirt, a waistcoat or handkerchief, in which case it is more than probable that he would have held his tongue. What he found were old papers, which he faithfully handed over to me. I don't blame him for that. I didn't blame him either on the day that I discovered that he helped himself to two or three coins a day each time he brushed my waistcoats. That was two months ago, and possibly it had been going on ever since he entered the house. I didn't tell him off; what I did was to keep an eye on my coins, but so that he should not know that he had been discovered I occasionally left one or two, some of which were promptly appropriated. Since I don't get angry he probably calls me names, like scatter-brain, fool, simpleton and so on. I bear him no ill will for his stealing and calling me names. He is fond of me and looks after me well; he could steal more and call me worse names.

I've made up my mind to have the papers burned whatever distress this causes José, who thought he had uncovered some precious relics of the past. I could explain that we all carry in

106

our heads old papers that never get burned and never get lost in battered old suitcases, but he wouldn't understand me.

Visiting cards in honour of my birthday are beginning to arrive, among them ones from the Aguiars, Tristão and Fidelia. The widow wrote these words: *Best wishes from a true friend.* And now I remember that when we met in Flamengo in the Aguiars' house on the 12th I had used the expression *true friend*, this being the closest relationship I could wish for. It was a way of winding up some discreet words in her praise in support of others proffered by Dona Carmo. Hence today's greeting. Tristão's message expressed admiration, that of the Aguiars affection and esteem. Rita hasn't written, so no doubt she will be coming to dinner.

Midnight

She came all right; Rita arrived for dinner in her usual high spirits and examined all the letters and cards. She explained that she had been to Flamengo yesterday and told them of my birthday; hence today's compliments.

On hearing that, I couldn't help asking about the letters that had been waiting for Tristão. She said that she knew about them and that they were from his parents and political friends. Among the first was one for Dona Carmo, with a postscript for her husband. After some hesitation I asked whether they were pressing for his return.

'Not his parents,' answered Rita. 'I don't know about his friends; I only heard from Dona Carmo that they wrote a lot about local politics. She sounded a little anxious and upset as if already alarmed at the prospect of his departure. But that's only natural.'

'Didn't Tristão say anything?'

'Not that I heard. I spent a good half-hour talking with them, and the principal subject was Tristão's visit to Santa-Pia, which he found interesting on account of its old customs. He enjoyed seeing the veranda, the old slaves' quarters, the well, the plantation and the bell. He even made sketches of some things. Fidelia listened to all this with great interest; she asked him questions and he replied.'

'Does she still intend to sell the fazenda?'

'They didn't say anything about that.'

'Oh, she'll sell it all right. At least that was the idea some time ago, and the Judge went there to take charge of the papers. When is he coming back?'

'They say in seven or eight days. Two weeks at the most.'

'Fidelia dined with them, of course?'

'No. When I left it was four o'clock. Carmo asked me to stay, but as I had to make another call I said I couldn't. Then Fidelia said she would take advantage of my company, and though Carmo insisted she stay for dinner she said she was expected at home and couldn't stay. She'd be back today or tomorrow. Carmo and Tristão went with us to the garden gate. Fidelia and I walked off together, and when we reached the corner of Rua da Princesa I forgot to look back. Fidelia didn't, so I followed her example and saw the two of them standing on the pavement waving goodbye.'

Rita told me that she went to Botafogo with Fidelia, and that on the way they spoke little, or rather it was Fidelia who spoke little; she seemed worried. Apart from this she was her usual self, affectionate, almost tender-hearted. She regretted their not having met more often and apologized for not having been to Andaraí for so long. If her words were few they were not lacking in warmth, just the contrary.

They naturally spoke of Dona Carmo and Aguiar and also mentioned Tristão, agreeing that he seemed very friendly with his godparents.

Near her uncle's house Fidelia entered a florist's shop to order the flowers she would take to her husband's grave on November 2nd. Rita, who had not yet thought of this, did not order hers but will do so nearer to All Souls' Day and bring them with her from the city. She described to me Fidelia's order, her choice of flowers, her requirements, the number of wreaths (three) and the combination of colours. She left nothing to the florist.

To all these details and even more I listened with great interest. I have always had a taste for observing character and how it expresses itself, and am rarely displeased by the way things fall out. I like to see, to foresee and to draw my own conclusions. This Fidelia of ours is running away from something, if she isn't running away from herself. I had in mind to say this to Rita, but in accordance with my old habit I thought twice before speaking and said nothing. My sister could upset the apple-cart. On the other hand I could be wrong.

I'll omit the rest. When she had finished and told of her return home I asked her why she hadn't come to have dinner with me yesterday. She answered that since she had to come today she didn't want a last-minute invitation. I laughed and we went to the table, which was already laid. In the centre was a bouquet of flowers, her idea, which she had sent secretly, and when I asked if they were the same as Fidelia had ordered she burst out laughing too. I thanked her for her kind thought with true brotherly affection, and we had a cheerful meal recalling our childhood days and family life.

18 October

When I got out of bed the first idea that came to me was what I had written at midnight: that girl (Fidelia) is running away from something, if she isn't running away from herself.

22 October

Fidelia didn't return to Flamengo despite the promise that Dona Carmo made her give, so the old lady went to see her and found her painting. Fidelia had remembered that she used to paint as a young girl, and was now at work on a corner of her garden. She promised to go to Flamengo the following day but did not go.

On learning the reason for her absence Tristão was convinced that Fidelia's talent for painting must be equal to that for music; I don't know whether he called it wonderful, he didn't say. What I write I had from the lad himself, and there are other things too I shall include on this page before I forget. He had come to have lunch with me.

'I've come to have lunch with you, Counsellor. I was just returning from my walk when I remembered to come up and ask how you were. Your servant said you were about to have lunch, so I make so bold as to beg a place at your table.'

'One place, two, three – for a friend, as many places as your appetite demands, Doctor,' I answered.

He gave me news of the Aguiars, who are well, and of his family and the political letters from Lisbon, which he has already read to his godparents. Only one expresses a wish for him to return soon: 'We hope you won't stay too long in Rio de Janeiro.'

'And do you intend to stay long?' I asked.

'I don't know, but it's not likely. The party wants me.'

It was over lunch that Tristão told me about the picture Fidelia is painting and of the promise to her friend that she didn't keep. Then he said, 'If she can really paint I thought that better than her garden would be a stretch of the sea front at Flamengo, for instance, with the mountains in the distance, the entrance to the bay, some islands, a boat and so on. Dona Carmo agreed with me and went there to suggest a change of subject. Fidelia liked the idea and promised to come to Flamengo to sketch it, but she never came.'

'She likes her own garden. And generally artists know best what appeals to them. Does she still know how to paint like she said she could when a child?'

'My godmother only saw a rough sketch, but it seemed to her to be good.'

We agreed that it must be good and, one thing leading to another, we discussed Fidelia's charm, her bearing, her discretion, her recollections of her travels, her good taste, her appearance, and I think we also mentioned her eyes. I certainly mentioned her eyes, and now I recall that he said they were both beautiful and sad. Giving his opinion or changing the subject, he added that in general his former countrywomen had beautiful eyes, and went on to speak at length of other ladies so as not to give the impression he was praising just Fidelia. I agreed with him, finding his observations both just and aesthetically sound. In the middle of our conversation an idea occurred to me: I said that since Dona Carmo was so fond of them both, instead of a simple picture of the beach she should suggest adding a human

110

figure to it. His own would be ideal as a memento for her when he was gone: the portrait of her son painted by her daughter.

Tristão smiled at this, and then repeated thoughtfully, 'The portrait of her son painted by her daughter.'

I won't describe his smile, which was a mixture of longing, hope and tenderness: I am no good at either description or painting. But it was exactly as I have just said, if those three words can convey an idea of the mixture, or unless the mixture had even more ingredients. From there we passed on to the art galleries of Europe and talked of our experiences, and before we knew it we had finished lunch. I offered him cigars and my heart – in other words I begged him to come again many times to give me another such pleasurable hour. He replied he wouldn't come to give but to receive, which I thought a graceful return of my compliment.

He said goodbye and left. I had intended to go out right away, but first, as I have already said, I came to write this down before I forget. And now I have written it I am confirmed in my original impression of the lad, which was good. He may be guilty of some dissimulation, as well of other defects of our society, but one has to be imperfect in this world of ours. There, now I'll go out, and tomorrow or the next day I'll go and find out more of this landscape or seascape of the beautiful Fidelia.

28 October

Seascape or landscape, I couldn't discover a thing. Fidelia hasn't been to Flamengo, and today she wrote a letter of apology to her old friend to say that she is going over her uncle's accounts; he returned yesterday from the fazenda. I don't remember if I've already mentioned that the Do Sul Bank is responsible for the sale of Santa-Pia.

Dona Carmo, on the pretext of admiring the style, gave me the letter to read. Naturally it is well written, but her real motive is the tenderness she feels in reading her friend's letter and in letting other people read it. After I returned it she read it again to herself. She must know it by heart by now. Amid all this she let me know that she liked my idea of having her son painted by her daughter, which Tristão had passed on to her.

'I must speak to Fidelia about it.'

Tristão was not there, having gone to dine with a minister. In my view it was easier for the girl to promise than to paint the seascape. And I don't think Dona Carmo will do what she said she would; she won't in fact ask Fidelia to come and add the portrait of her godson to her seascape of Flamengo. Whatever familiarity there may exist between them, it would hardly extend to this which, even in the name of art, might be considered unseemly or I don't know what else. . . .

At this point I will lay down my pen and go to bed. I'll report on the rest of the evening tomorrow.

29 October

The rest of the evening I spent at Faria's house. It was his birthday, and I stayed there longer than I intended. There was a cheerful crowd there, with some singing, piano playing and plenty of conversation.

Although it was his birthday Faria's gaiety was forced, artificial, constrained; I can't find words to express exactly what it was. Surly and unforthcoming, he is a born bore. His wife, Dona Cesaria, was as bright and witty as ever, and if she didn't speak ill of anyone it was for lack of time, not material, or so it seemed to me. Any material serves for those with sharp tongues. The almost sarcastic manner in which she stirs up scandal is not easily understood by those who do not have the skill and aptitude of such creatures; myself, for instance, old gossip-monger that I am. Or am I just the opposite, who knows? The next rainy day I must settle down to some self-analysis.

When I left Faria expressed his pleasure in what can only be called his gruff, nasal accents, and gave me a fleeting gaoler's smile.

1 November

Today is All Saints' Day, and tomorrow All Souls'. The Church is quite right to appoint a day to remember those who have passed away. . . . In the rough and tumble of life, one day is set aside for them. . . . The reticence which can be observed here is an indication of the effort I made to terminate this page in a melancholy mood. But I can't; I never could. Gloom is not for me. Yet, as a young lad, when I wrote verse it was always of the most tragic kind. The tears I shed then, black because my ink was black, would have flooded the whole world – this world, which is their valley!

2 November

My sister Rita went to the cemetery today with flowers to lay on the family graves.

'Do you know, I got up at half-past five so as to be dressed and arrive early at São João Batista. I arrived just after eight and found lots of people there, but not so many as there will be later this afternoon. I didn't come for you because I knew you wouldn't go.'

'I went to mass at Gloria Church.'

'That's nearby.'

'I might have gone to the cemetery. Were there many beautiful graves?'

'Quite a few, among them Fidelia's husband's. The wreaths and flowers she ordered the other day were prettily laid out and looked most attractive. It seems the Judge sent flowers too, I saw his name on a ribbon.'

'Did you speak to her?'

'No, she had already left.'

'So how do you know that she took the flowers and wreaths herself?'

'You can tell by the way they were laid out.'

'Can you?'

'My dear brother, of course you can. The layout, the arrangement, the combination, it was all done by a woman. There are things a man can't do; a man's hand is too heavy and clumsy, especially if it happens to be a judge's, like him. Take her husband's name, for instance; the Christian name, not the whole name, was enclosed in evergreens – that's something only a woman would think of and do. The other flowers, roses and poppies, were so beautifully laid out, and with such good taste, that it must have taken a long time. A man would just go there, grab the flowers and scatter them about anyhow.'

'I'm surprised you didn't see her.'

'She left very early.'

'But a day like today, and with so much to arrange. That time we saw her it was much later.'

'I know it was, but today was different. Today there were a lot of people and she didn't want to be seen, that's what it was.'

Rita developed this idea, which I accepted as reasonable, and then went on to describe other graves. From the graves we passed on to the Ministry, then to Dona Cesaria, why I'm not quite sure, but we spoke of both with interest and my sister quite wittily. The two women had met yesterday afternoon, when Rita had apologized for not going there on the 28th. She recounted part of what she had heard concerning two people who were there. . . .

'Who were there?'

'It seems so.'

She then repeated a series of tales and gossip which I listened to attentively for ten minutes. Spreading scandal is not such a bad habit as it seems. For an idle or empty mind, or one which is both these, it provides a useful occupation. And then the aim of proving that others are good for nothing, if not always justified, very often is, and to be once right is to justify all the rest. I said this to Rita in the most charming way possible, but she was not amused and attributed it to my perverse nature.

9 November

The seascape has interrupted the landscape, or at least caused it to be laid aside. Fidelia agreed to go and paint a stretch of the sea front at Flamengo, though with or without Tristão I'm not sure. Aguiar gave me the news, merely adding that she had already begun the picture and was very enthusiastic.

'Go there tomorrow, Counsellor, between one and two o'clock.'

11 November

I didn't go there yesterday to see the seascape, I went today. Fidelia was in the garden, near the house, with brush and palette in her hands, her eyes fixed on the sea and the canvas standing beside her. Seated nearby was Dona Carmo, with her broad, motherly smile. On seeing me at the garden gate she waved to me to enter, so I did.

'Come and see my artist,' she said.

Fidelia seemed embarrassed by these words, but she laid down her brush and offered me her hand, saying, 'Don't look. You mustn't look, it's no good.'

I did look, and it was good. It is still just the outline, and will be no masterpiece, but politeness required me to pronounce it excellent. I said so, with a gesture of admiration, but it really is good. The mountains and the sky make an effective background, while the sea I thought had colour and movement. There was no Tristão, no shadow of 'the son painted by the daughter'. Though his absence did not surprise me, I decided to drop a hint. I suggested that on the beach she might include the figure of her friend, who was sitting watching her at work with her loving eyes.

Dona Carmo was about to say something, but Fidelia answered, 'I didn't dare. I've no experience of figure drawing. At school we just painted flowers and landscapes, the sea and the sky. Otherwise I'd have drawn Dona Carmo's portrait.'

Dona Carmo confirmed this: 'I asked her to include Tristão in the picture and she said the same thing.'

I accepted her argument, also accepting an empty chair which was there, and begged Fidelia to continue with her work. I wanted to see her painting. In Europe I had watched men painters at work but this was the first time a woman had painted before me. She picked up her things and returned to her work. After a few moments we were all three deep in conversation. Fidelia was as graceful as usual, painting modestly, with no artificial posing on account of her occupation. Sometimes she would pause in her work either to listen better or to speak at greater length, and then return to her brush and her canvas.

After some minutes I was beginning to think of leaving them when who should appear at the door of the house but Tristão himself. It is a wide door, giving on to a porch, which is reached by two short flights of covered steps. Tristão had just finished writing the letters he was putting in the post, as I discovered later, and was returning to re-occupy his place beside the two women. He sent for a chair as the one I was sitting on had been his and there was no other. These details may be insignificant, but I record them to emphasize that Tristão had been with them before my arrival, and to remember that before the chair came he asked my opinion of the picture. I gave a suitable reply.

'Isn't that so?' he said, pleased with my approval.

He added some further words of praise, warm and no doubt sincere, which Fidelia accepted quite naturally. She did not refute them, neither did she smile as happens when we silently approve words that touch the heart. She painted while listening, stepping back or moving in closer and gazing out into the distance. When she turned her eyes on Tristão (already seated by now) she did not wait for him to avert his, but met and held them, and then went on with her painting, so absorbed in it that it was as if we were not talking at all. And in fact we were all busy talking, he perhaps less in order to see the picture better.

That silence of Fidelia's, in contrast with her earlier loquacity, seemed to me to indicate that she felt she was getting behindhand with her work. Or it might have been that her love of art now operated more strongly than at the beginning, causing her to dedicate herself exclusively to her painting. The hidden reasons for an action frequently escape even the sharpest eyes, and especially mine, which with age have lost their natural sharpness. But I think one of those was the cause, and there is no reason to doubt that it could be both one and the other, successively.

The one who seemed delighted with everything, conversation and silences, was the lady of the house. Although her attentions were principally directed towards me, she did not permit herself to forget the picture and the young people. She gazed at it and spoke to them with that tenderness that I am weary of noting down, and perhaps this was greater than at other times. At any rate it had an intensity as of one who begins to sense a new and unexpected source of happiness. I'll say no more in case I should be mistaken.

The truth is that I, who had been on the point of leaving, lingered on, and went on lingering until Fidelia gave up for the day. Almost an hour had passed. Saying that she was tired, she began gathering together her brushes and covering the picture, helped in this by Tristão, who did so as gracefully as she, and with a sincere wish to be of service, which is the soul of courtesy. I, being old, could not leave Dona Carmo, whose only assistance was with her eyes, and very effective it was; they moved from one to the other, not merely happy, but pensive too. The two finished what they had to do and came to sit down in front of us, he full of smiles, she less so, but not unmoved by the sincerity and gratitude expressed in his.

My visit was now over-extended, and despite the intimacy between us was verging on the indiscreet. It was time to go. I wanted to leave and stay at the same time, which was impossible, and I remained a few moments torn between opposing impulses. Tristão might have resolved this internal struggle for me by bringing up some subject that would oblige me to listen to him, but at that moment he was occupied in paying compliments to the artist, the widow, the sister, to those three persons in one that made up that enchanting young lady, Fidelia. She was listening to him, smiling shyly when she answered. I said goodbye and had the impression (if I wasn't mistaken) that Dona Carmo was glad to see me go so as to devote herself entirely to her two children. It is nonetheless true, however, that all three were most polite in their farewell. I came away with them still in my thoughts.

12 November

I ought to have written down the thoughts that I brought away with me yesterday. I think Tristão has fallen in love with Fidelia. When I was a lad we used to say *lovestruck*; it was more forceful, though without the grace and spirituality of the other expression. 'To make love' is banal, it gives the idea of an occupation for the idle or licentious, but 'fall in love' is more expressive. 'Band of lovers' brings to mind the knights of olden times who did battle for their ladies. . . . Those were the days!

My impression is that, if he hasn't already, he is beginning to fall in love with the girl. Another impression which I did not write either, is that his godmother suspects as much and is overjoyed. When I go there again I shall have to have all my wits about me to confirm or disprove these two impressions. I might be mistaken, but I might also be right.

Today, since I'm not going out, I'll note down these ideas. In doing so I bow to the necessity of talking to myself, since I cannot do so with other people; that's my trouble. By nature and habit I am a talkative person. Diplomatic life gave me the patience to put up with the countless intolerable creatures that for some mysterious reason of her own this world nurtures. Retirement turned me back upon myself, but there come days when, not being able to go out, and tired of reading, I am obliged to talk, and not wishing to talk to myself, I write.

13 November

Aguiar came to me and said, 'I hear you liked the seascape.'
   'Very much. Is it getting along well?'
   'Oh yes.'
   'The artist hasn't given up then?'
   'No, she goes there every day. It's a labour of love.'
   'Love? That is her driving force. I don't know whether I ever told you, but what most touches me about the affection she has for you both, and particularly for Dona Carmo, is that charming submissiveness which makes her seem so completely like a daughter. It is the discreet way in which she implicitly obeys the wishes of those whom she regards as her parents.'
   'You put it very well, Counsellor.'
   We were leaving the Treasury, having gone there on business, and were walking to Rocio to pick up a tram, but we didn't pick up anything. Conversation was our best means of transport; its wheels are silent and rapid and it carries you along without any jolts. We pursued the subject while we walked, saying the most interesting things, or at least I did because he exercised his eyes and ears more than his tongue. He listened attentively, sometimes inattentively, and in the second case he was gazing about so distractedly that he forgot his street and his companion.
   One of his confidences is worth mentioning here. To give an instance of what I had called Fidelia's charming submissiveness, he told me that the two used to go to mass at Gloria Church on Sundays, Fidelia coming to meet Dona Carmo at Flamengo, after which she would return to Botafogo if she didn't stay for lunch.

'To save her such a long journey, some Sundays Carmo would go to Botafogo for mass, but almost always it was Fidelia who came to Gloria.'

'And now she doesn't come any more?'

'No, it's Carmo who doesn't go to either place, or only very rarely. She is very tired, poor thing, and she has her missal at home with all the prayers marked. On Sundays, at the same time as in church, before looking at the papers, she betakes herself to her missal and follows the whole mass. Knowing the time, I never disturb her, and if I should unwittingly walk into the room where she has her tiny altar and her image of Christ, I back out again without her ever lifting her eyes from the page. It's as if no one had entered. She finishes, kisses the image, and returns to this world. She never leaves the house without kissing it first, as if begging protection, and does the same on her return, still in her coat and hat, as a thanksgiving. It's the same thing when she goes to bed and when she gets up.'

Aguiar told me more of his wife's day-to-day habits, besides these, which I listened to with pleasure. Not that they are all that interesting, but I am one of those persons who find pleasure in the smallest things provided they are sincere. I wouldn't admit this to anyone face to face, but to you my journal, who hear me patiently and sometimes approvingly, to you my dear old friend I can and will confess myself, cost what it may, and it costs me nothing. I believe other ladies say mass at home, either because they are tired, or ill, or because it is raining, and there is always something to be admired in people who so respect their spiritual links. I am only annoyed by those who do so merely to improve their own image. That sweet old lady in Flamengo is not one of these. Her piety extends to the memory of her mother and father, her feeling for her friends and (though I am tired of repeating it) her affection for her adopted children.

20 November

I have been back there three times. On each occasion I found Dona Carmo, Fidelia and Tristão, and on the third Aguiar arrived early in time to watch the last strokes of the brush.

119

Yes, I think the lad admires the painting less than the artist, or the artist more than the painting, whichever you prefer. One hypothesis or the other, what is certain is that he is in love. He has reached the point of forgetting all about us, being solely taken up by her, absorbed in her, carried away by her. I, with the art the Devil granted me, divided my attentions between the mother and the two children, in order to satisfy, successfully, the demands of both politeness and curiosity.

When I wrote the other day (two or three times) that 'Fidelia is running away from something, if she isn't running away from herself', I was referring to her non-appearance at her friend's house. But now she has taken up going there again, letting herself be seen by the brother that her friend provided for her. Either she no longer wishes to run away from him, or (more serious) she no longer wishes to run away from herself. I haven't fully understood it; her mood seems more that of resignation.

30 November

Tristão invited me to go up to Paineiras with him tomorrow and I accepted.

Ten days now without writing anything. Not through illness or any kind of indisposition or laziness. Neither is it lack of material, just the contrary. During this time I learned that fresh letters have arrived for Tristão, formally urging his return to Europe on account of the forthcoming elections, though the matter is not pressing yet. Tristão decided not to go before the beginning of the year, but sooner or later he'll have to go. That was the news I picked up in Flamengo and other places. I also heard it from the lips of the charming Cesaria, who said sadly, 'He likes Fidelia, but it's obvious that he likes politics more.'

It was the sadness of secret pleasure, or whatever phrase might serve to describe a witty conceit that has to be disguised as sorrow. Her words suggested a certain condemnation of the young man, but only on the surface; the real meaning was her pleasure at seeing the girl rejected. In order to disguise this she spoke all the ill she knows of the lad, which is not a little. She did so as charmingly as ever, with her biting observations and elegant manners. Naturally I laughed, whether arguing with her or holding my tongue. I felt deep down that she was being unjust, but this may be due to the affection I have for the lad. This has grown as our acquaintance has developed, and naturally with the affection and trust he has, or seems to have in me. Be that as it may, I did not defend him entirely, only in part, and the gracious lady appealed to my good taste, my well-balanced mind, the long experience I have of men . . . all the finest qualities in the world.

1 December

I have just returned from Paineiras, where a surprise lay in store for me. I went there with Tristão today. After lunch, high up above the city and the sea, I heard no less than his confession of the love he dedicates the beautiful Fidelia. Those are his own words: dedicates the beautiful Fidelia. The verb, though maybe elegant, is inexpressive, but at least it indicates the singleness of its object. School exercises are dedicated to parents, relatives and friends; love is an exercise for a single person.

This in itself was nothing new, it was the confession that astonished me, and probably this was what he read in my face. I did not reply immediately other than with a gesture of approval, always necessary in such cases for one must never doubt the wisdom of the other's choice, just the contrary.

'I haven't told this to anyone, Counsellor, not even to my godmother or godfather. And if I'm telling you now it is because I haven't the courage to tell them, and I have no third person whom I can. I might have spoken to your sister, had I dared, but though she is kind hearted I don't find her so open and frank as you. Do you think I have chosen well?'

'An idle question, Doctor. To be in love is to choose well. No matter who the devil you choose, your choice would be a good one.'

'As a general rule, I know. But in the case of this particular lady, don't you think she is an admirable person?'

'I do.'

'I think so too. And quite apart from the blindness which my passion may induce, I am convinced that my choice is an ideal one. We have talked of her before and always been of the same opinion. And I'll go so far as to say that that was the reason which prompted me to speak to you today. Do you remember some time ago when we were having lunch in your house . . . ? We agreed that she was admirable in every way, in character and appearance? I felt that you would approve, so I decided to speak to you about my feelings and their consequences.'

'As you say, the answer was already given: there was no need for a further consultation.'

'Oh but there is. I haven't told you everything.'

'Well, tell me the rest. I'll listen to you as if I were a young man myself. Have you been in love with her for long?'

'It began shortly after I arrived.'

'I didn't notice.'

'Neither did she, nor I myself. I realized I felt something for her, but with her being a widow and me returning shortly to Lisbon I didn't understand what it was. It might be just one of those attractions you feel towards women when there is no intention or possibility of it being taken any further. More than that, I enjoyed hearing her talk, and sharing with her my own ideas and observations – all our conversations were interesting. Everything about her attracted me – her manners, that calm, gentle way she has of expressing her agreement. One day I started thinking about her so insistently that I began to have my suspicions. You remember when I decided to go to Santa-Pia fazenda with her and her uncle?'

'Yes, I remember.'

'It was the idea of having to stay here without her, who knows for how long. And then I imagined that on the fazenda, more on our own, I'd be able to make her understand what I felt and persuade her to listen to me. It was a waste of time: she didn't go and I had to accompany the Judge on my own. I came back shortly afterwards . . .'

'I remember.'

At this point Tristão paused and gazed out into the distance. A waiter brought us coffee, while two huge, black birds glided through the air, one chasing the other. They might be a mating couple, he pursuing, she rebuffing. Then, in a light-hearted manner, I suggested that the beautiful Fidelia might be doing the same as the fleeing bird; perhaps she was already in love with him. He answered neither yes nor no, but the expression on his face was negative, so in order not to lose the rest of his story, I asked, 'But what makes you think she doesn't, Doctor?'

My curiosity was getting the better of my discretion, and perhaps of good manners too. It wasn't just curiosity, there was a touch of slyness in it as well. There's many a young man has spoken about his lady-love, and many a widow has ceased to be a widow, or has remained one. In this case the two people involved gave the affair a special interest. And I remembered my sister Rita's declaration that Fidelia would not marry. That she would never marry. The situations of both of them – the life which calls Tristão away, and the death which binds the widow here with her memories – were intriguing enough, even excluding the fact that to these arguments in favour of their separation, I myself could add others in favour of their possible union.

Tristão was not hard to persuade, and recounted several of his mistakes and disappointments. It was not easy for him to begin with but after the first instance came others, and before long I learned that appearances had given him false hopes and that disappointments had killed them stone dead. Now he truly believes the worst.

I didn't give him any of my theories to the contrary as they too might be based on no more than appearances. Neither did I allude to the imagined suspicions of his godparents who, like me, could be wrong. For the rest – and this was the most important thing – I assumed my role with less despair than the circumstances warranted. It was something that our conversation had opened his heart, and mine too, and by the time we had finished our cigars we were like two first-year students discussing their first love affairs, though with considerably more style.

On our way back I felt he was regretting his confession, or embarrassed by it. He changed the subject, and we talked of other matters, the train and the road, the woods and the mountain, and once down here in the city again, something of the politics of both countries.

One point of interest. How is it that Tristão was so frank yesterday in Paineiras and so circumspect that day in Largo de São Francisco when I saw him all agape watching the girl get into the cab? 'A wonderful talent!' he exclaimed then, meaning her musical talent, something she didn't carry around under her skirts. And yet, according to what he said yesterday, by then he was already in love with her since it all began shortly after his arrival. The reason is that only now has his passion reached this pitch; this, and the confidence he feels in me. He wasn't able to restrain himself, that's what it was.

Aires, my old friend, confess that when you heard of Tristão's grief at not being loved, though it was of short duration and not repeated, you felt just a tiny thrill of pleasure. You don't want her for yourself, but it would smart to think that she was in love with him. Explain yourself if you can, but you can't. Later you came down to earth and saw that there is no divine law forbidding them happiness, if they both wish to seek it together. It is a question of her loving him, and she, it seems, does not.

The seascape is almost finished. Rita came here delighted with the picture, the artist and the owner, for Fidelia is giving it to Dona Carmo. She was alone with just the two friends, neither Tristão nor Aguiar being there, and the three had a long chat until Fidelia said goodbye and left for Botafogo. She was urged to stay for dinner at Flamengo, but said she couldn't and left before it turned dark.

Rita stayed on and it was as well she did for she learned from Dona Carmo of Tristão's love for Fidelia, with an addition that ties in well with what I have been writing these last few days. This is none other than Dona Carmo's wish to see them married.

'I haven't told anyone but you,'said Dona Carmo, 'and I beg you not to mention it to anyone else. I would like to see them married because they are so well suited and because they are both my dear friends as I am theirs.'

Rita believed not only that she was speaking the truth, but that she saw their marriage as a means of keeping her godson here. Being one of those people who have to say what they think, my sister said as much to her friend. Dona Carmo smiled her agreement, and it was as she had suspected, Rita told me. That too was my opinion, but with my usual caustic humour I added, 'Maybe the third reason is the main one, or indeed the only one.'

Rita was quick to deny it. It wasn't the only one, it couldn't be. Out of perversity and to amuse myself I insisted it was, but deep down I had to admit she was right. For Dona Carmo all three reasons were valid, and the third gave greater weight to the other two, as was only natural. She was about to lose her godson, who was going away, while her adopted daughter might well fall in love with another, marry and, though without going away, attach herself to another family. With the two of them together here, finding themselves beloved, she would have them close to her heart and would die happy. That is what I thought then, and I confirm it now, only adding that I said as much to my sister.

'I was only joking when I said that just now. I think you are right. But do you think there is any chance she will succeed?'

'I can't say one way or the other, but I doubt it, and this is why. Tristão and Aguiar arrived just before dinner, and we all dined together. Aguiar and Dona Carmo talked about the painting, he asking questions and listening to her answers with interest. From time to time they glanced at their godson, but Tristão never spoke and seemed uninterested in what they were saying.'

'Perhaps he was pretending.'

'After dinner, just before coffee, Tristão told them that he may be leaving before the end of the year.'

'Before?'

'Before.'

'And they didn't know?'

'It seems not because they were very upset. It was a sad ending to the dinner.'

'But how was it he didn't say anything to his godfather since he came back to the house with him?'

'They didn't come back together, Tristão arrived after Aguiar. We even thought that he was having dinner out. That's how it was, he simply said he was leaving. He said that he had just had a letter . . . but he didn't show it. He must have done so after I left.'

I pondered the matter, and then said, 'You know, Rita, there's probably no letter at all. He's running away from her. He has given up hope and wants to leave as soon as he can. His arriving home late proves that he doesn't want to meet Fidelia, that's what it is. Didn't the two of them try to dissuade him?'

'At first they said nothing, they were too overwhelmed. Then Aguiar said something, and Dona Carmo gazed at him pleadingly. She looked miserable, but so as not to leave me out of it she spoke to me, and I squeezed her fingers to show how sorry I felt. I even spoke up myself to ask him to stay a little longer, but he just gave a sad smile of gratitude and said that he couldn't as they were pressing him to return.'

'Well,' I said, with a laugh, 'you've just said that you felt sorry for your friend, Dona Carmo. It's only December yet you seem already to have forgotten the bet you made with me at the beginning of January. Don't you remember what you said to me in the cemetery? Didn't you bet that Noronha's widow would never marry again? So how could you today ask Tristão to stay – secretly hoping that he would marry her?'

I was standing above her, and with my last words I seized her chin and raised her face to me. She admitted the contradiction and gave her explanation. First and foremost her idea had been to lessen her friend's grief, for it would mean extra days or weeks that they would be able to spend together with their godson. But it was also possible that Fidelia, on their advice, would end up marrying Tristão. The circumstances were different.

'So I was right that day?'

'Not entirely, but anything can happen in this world.'

'In this world and the next.'

I was tempted to end the conversation by pointing out that in spite of Dona Carmo's request for secrecy when she disclosed her hidden hopes, Rita had just revealed everything to me. But I hadn't the heart to tease her with it, no matter in how brotherly or innocent a manner it was done. She might feel hurt, and she doesn't deserve that. She's a good soul.

In short, Rita may have been right in the cemetery. If, as I wrote some days ago, Fidelia is running away from herself, it is because she is afraid of falling, and prefers her widowhood to the alternative.

10 December

Fidelia already knows that Tristão has decided to leave on the 24th. He told her himself in her house.

15 December

If I was sure of being able to marry the two of them I'd do so, cost what it may, this confession to myself, and to be honest it doesn't cost much. I am alone within these four walls, and with my sixty-three years I don't reject the idea of the ecclesiastical function. *Ego conjugo vobis.* . . .

This feeling was prompted by seeing the growing sorrow of the godparents as the 24th draws nearer. Dona Carmo begged to know why he couldn't postpone his journey until the 9th of January, which would give him another fortnight. He replied that he couldn't. Somewhat incredulous, I asked him if he had already bought his ticket, and he told us that he is going to buy it tomorrow. I suspect that his idea is to wait in the hope that all the tickets will be sold, thus causing him to postpone his journey through *force majeure*. I didn't say so, but anything is to be expected of one's fellow men, particularly when they are in love.

It was yesterday when the three of us talked about this; Aguiar was with us but he gave no opinion. A little later Campos arrived with his niece; they had been to visit the President of the Tribunal, and it was only when they were in the street that Fidelia had suggested they come and spend the evening at Flamengo. It was nine o'clock when they arrived.

Everything that happened between then and half-past ten would merit three or four pages here if it weren't that my fingers are too tired. Pages full of conjectures, because the two barely spoke, but conjectures confirmed by the agitation they both displayed, and by Fidelia's silence, only interrupted by the attentions she paid her friend. The ice was slow to break among us four men. Campos even suggested a game of cards but none of us accepted. Aguiar was about to, somewhat timidly, but Tristão alleged he had a headache, or a backache, which was true since he had spent all the morning bending down sorting out old odds and ends. The tiredness in my fingers now is what remains of the weariness I felt yesterday. We stayed talking until the two visitors left, and I with them.

20 December

It happened exactly as I had foreseen. Tristão found all the tickets for the 24th sold. He is going on the 9th. The funny thing is that although the obvious thing to do would be to buy his ticket right away so as not to have the same thing happen again, he has not done so. He told me so himself when I asked him if he had already taken this precaution, replying that there was plenty of time. And now I suppose that if there is time and he manages to get a ticket he will convert his need to court the lady into the wish to please his godparents and stay for another two or three weeks. The old folk may not be the real cause, but just as there are adopted children so there are adopted causes.

22 December

The real cause – or one of them – was at Flamengo today finishing her seascape. Tristão was there too, and both were lost in the appreciation of the other. He admired less the painting than the artist, she less the scenery than the admirer, while I contemplated both with these eyes of mine that will soon be consigned to the cold earth.

Dona Carmo gave me the attention that courtesy required, but no more than that. She threw frequent glances at the two, observing them attentively, ready to encourage them if necessary. But it was no longer necessary. They were in a world of their own, carried along to the sound of that music of the heart to which she was no stranger.

Looking at the girl then, I thought of what they had told me a week ago, of the idea she had had to spend the summer at

128

Santa-Pia, which is still unsold. She would not have minded staying there with her freed slaves, but there was no one to keep her company. Just lately she had thought of going to Petropolis, but it was likely that Tristão would go there too, and as I understood it her intention was to avoid him. I believe too that she was sincere in both her projects. At the door of her heart Fidelia heard that other heart beating, and it was her whim to lock it out. I say whim because these do not have the force of obligation. The person herself wants something quite different, the opposite in fact, and her own feelings, if not already all-powerful, urge her in that direction.

One impression that I brought away from Flamengo is that when I got up, Dona Carmo said goodbye to me with the same pleasure as she had done some days ago when I left her alone with the two of them. She will not have said anything to them in words, but as far as she could express herself without words, I have no doubt she did. Only her sense of decorum would prevent her from taking them in her arms and saying, 'Love each other, my children!'

28 December

I was with Tristão today, but he said nothing except that he has received letters from Lisbon, some on political business and others from his mother and father. His mother says that if he delays much longer she will come and pay a visit to her native land. He gave me news of his godparents, but said nothing of the girl.

1889

2 January

They're in love! Fidelia fled from him and from herself as long as she could, but she can do so no longer. Now she belongs to him, laughs with him, and on the 9th will naturally weep for him unless he does the needful to prevent her tears. They visit each other every day now and dine together frequently. Dona Carmo sometimes accompanies her godson to Botafogo and Aguiar goes there to fetch them.

What I don't know is whether or not they are formally engaged. Perhaps he has not yet found the opportunity or the courage to declare what her own eyes can tell her, but it can't be long now. That is what I infer from my own observations and conjectures, and principally from the joy on the faces of the Aguiars. My sister hasn't left the house. On New Year's Day I had dinner with her but we didn't speak of these matters.

7 January

Tristão is not sailing on the 9th; he didn't say why not and I didn't ask him. All he said was that he is not sailing. He had written to Lisbon and was on his way to the post with the letters.

9 January

Today is the second anniversary of my coming back to Rio for good. I didn't hear the street cries as I had done last year and the year before. This time I remembered the date with no sounds from outside; it came of its own accord. I expected my sister to call by to invite me to go with her to the cemetery. She hasn't come (it is 4 p.m.) either because she has forgotten or because she doesn't consider it necessary every year.

Who knows, we might have met Fidelia beside her husband's grave, with folded hands, praying as she did a year ago. If I still had the same impression which led me to bet with Rita that she would marry again, I believe I might find pleasure in seeing her there and in that attitude. I might take it as a sign that she doesn't love Tristão, and since I can't marry her I would prefer her to love her dead husband. But no, that's not true. What I mean is this. Even if I saw her there and in that same posture I still wouldn't doubt her love for Tristão. All this could exist in the same person without hypocrisy on the part of the widow or infidelity on the part of the future wife. It was the reconciliation or the conflict between the individual and the species. The memory of the dead man lives on in her without prejudicing the claims of the lover; it lives on in all its former sweetness and sorrow, and in those secrets of a heart that learned its first lessons with him. But the genius of the species resurrects him in another human form, delivering him to her with its blessing. While she could fly, she did, as I wrote some days ago, and repeat now so as never to forget it.

12 January

Tomorrow (the 13th) is the birthday of the beautiful Fidelia. This was the reason Tristão postponed his departure from the 9th to some other date he hasn't yet fixed. That is what he told his godparents, who naturally gave their joyful approval, and that is what he told me when I met him today looking for a memento to leave her. Those were his words, but they didn't sound very convincing. There is another reason for him staying.

13 January

Before I undress I want to write down what I heard just now (midnight) from the sharp-tongued Cesaria. We had been to the Judge's house to have tea with the charming Fidelia, and I came away with her and her husband. The Aguiars and Tristão were there, but not Rita, who sent a card; it seems she is not well.

I'm not writing what Dona Cesaria told me because it's true, but because it's spiteful. If this lady didn't have her touch of malice she'd likely be of no interest, but I never see her without it, and it's delightful. Either she already knew about Fidelia being in love with Tristão or she learned of it tonight. However it was, she told me that Tristão won't be leaving so soon for Lisbon.

'No,' I agreed, 'it seems he's not anxious to leave his god-parents.'

'His godparents?' retorted Cesaria, with a laugh. 'Really, Counsellor! Unless that's what you call the widow's two eyes, which make very bad godparents. But they have plenty of holy water for the christening.'

Not understanding her I asked what she meant by holy water and christening. Her husband, with his usual surliness, rubbed his thumb and forefinger together and answered that holy water meant money. She laughed her agreement, and I realized that they attributed Tristão's affection to self-interest.

I wanted to point out that what she said now was in contradiction to what I had once heard her state. She said then (and I think I wrote it in this journal) that Tristão preferred politics to the widow, which was the reason he was leaving her. I didn't remind her of this for two reasons. Firstly because it would do no good and might prejudice our relationship; secondly because it would be to condemn her very nature. Dona Cesaria really believes the evil she speaks. The contradiction is apparent, and is to be explained by the hatred she has for Fidelia. This sentiment is the true and only reason for her two conflicting opinions. Rejected on account of politics, or accepted on account of money, either way is to disparage the lady. To these two reasons why I heard her in silence must be added her manner of speaking. Her words are relatively sweet sounding and sincere, the venom or secret motive being well disguised. There are times when Dona Cesaria's charm is such that you feel it is a pity that what she says is not true, and it is easy to forgive her.

Everything considered, including the late hour, the shortness of the journey and the presence of her husband, what the deuce did I stand to gain by contradicting her? As soon as they left me

I began thinking about Tristão, who is rich himself, sincerely in love with Fidelia, is loved by her and will end up marrying her. I walked home recalling the events of the evening, which I won't note down now as it is too late, but they were interesting. It seems that the Judge has discovered his niece's feelings and does not disapprove. The Aguiars were happy, and stayed on to return with their godson.

23 January

I've just remembered that tomorrow is exactly a year since the Aguiars' silver wedding. I went to their party, which was a small, intimate one, and enjoyed myself very much. Fidelia was there too, and like a daughter proposed Dona Carmo's health; everyone was happy. Tristão had not yet arrived, nor was he even expected. I mustn't forget to send them a card right away offering my congratulations, and perhaps I'll go there in the evening. Yes, I'll definitely go.

... Rita has just written (6 p.m.) asking me to wait for her tomorrow evening so that we can go to Flamengo together. I'll go; it's six days since I set foot there.

25 January

There weren't many people at Flamengo. The four of them – the Aguiars, Tristão and Fidelia (I don't count the Judge, who was playing cards) – all four seemed to be secretly enjoying some new, anxiously awaited development. Who knows if the widow's hand has not already been solicited and granted. I mentioned this supposition to Rita, who said that she suspected as much too.

29 January

We were both right that evening of the 24th. The engagement is confirmed. Fidelia's hand was asked for that very day on account of it being the twenty-sixth wedding anniversary of Tristão's godparents. The request was made in her uncle's house in Botafogo, in his presence. She gave her consent and the uncle agreed, naturally having nothing to object to in the union of two young people in love. That is how everything ought to be settled, with everyone in agreement, everyone in harmony.

133

That evening Dona Carmo and Aguiar, who had hugged Tristão warmly before and after his proposal, were in their seventh heaven of delight. I swear to God they seemed even happier than the young couple. Fidelia, because of the duality of her situation, tried at first to moderate her happiness, but she forgot occasionally, and by the end of the evening, completely. No one knew of this development then, and even now I think I am the only one who knows for sure (as Tristão himself told me today). Others might have suspected, like my sister Rita, who knew half the story, while the less perspicacious, seeing them together, probably thought it was a good thing for Fidelia to help throw off her low spirits.

When he gave me this account of what happened five days ago, Tristão explained that he felt under an obligation to describe the end of the idyll, whose beginning he had related in the form of an elegy. He used these two expressions, and only stopped short of quoting Theocritus. It was with sincere pleasure that I shook him by the hand and promised to say nothing.

Indeed I am overjoyed to see them united. I have already written that it was a way to assuage the Aguiars' sorrow. Now I can add (if I haven't already done so) that they are ideally suited; they are young, handsome, in love, and have the natural and legitimate right to belong to each other.

'We are not going to make any official announcement of our forthcoming marriage,' concluded Tristão, 'because I have written to my parents, and we shall only marry after I have received their reply. Their answer is a foregone conclusion, but even if they refused their consent we should marry anyway. However, I don't want to make any announcement just yet out of respect for them.'

Next he treated me to a long account of Fidelia's excellent qualities. I had already heard him mention some, and I knew them all, but with people in his condition one needs all the indulgence one can muster. His sincerity and pleasure were such that it would have been cruel not to give him a sympathetic ear and words of encouragement. I did so, whereupon he concluded by requesting the first embrace from someone not of the family. I hugged him warmly.

The embrace I have just mentioned did me good; it was sincere. It could have been affected or merely given out of politeness, but it wasn't. I was pleased to see that lad happy, and with him his lady, as well as the two old people, both those here and those over there in Portugal.

I may be wrong, but it seems to me that Fidelia looks even prettier now, probably the result of the forthcoming change in her situation. Her former melancholy was sincere, but was like a stranger or guest in the house, I don't know quite how to describe it, a kind of visit of condolence – of short duration and few words. Three weeks ago, on the 9th of last month, I wrote something which in a way explains and reconciles her dual situation.

Nothing gets divulged quite so quickly as a close secret. Apart from myself, who know, and Rita, who suspects, there are others who declare that the two will marry, either because they know or because they merely suspect, but they declare it nonetheless. Osorio, when he heard of it, received a fresh, unexpected blow. And there will be no shortage of others in love with her, or sighing for her, who will consign Tristão to the Devil.

The truth is that Osorio had already been disillusioned, but now this came to open the wound. The cause of his original disillusionment was her fidelity to her late husband, but since she is giving herself to another, why not to him? This is what stings, just like when a backgammon player throws the dice and turns up the worst possible number.

Happiness loosens our tongues. Dona Carmo has not yet told me that the two are to be married, but today she informed me that she has written to her friend, Tristão's mother, whom she has not written to for a long time. In fact it went by the same boat that carried her godson's letter. Naturally she must have supported his request and given a favourable opinion of all Fidelia's virtues, and if she didn't ask her to allow them to stay here and come over herself, that is how it will turn out. Then, or before then, she'll tell me the rest.

I was intending to go and spend a month in Petropolis, but I found such pleasure in observing the progress of the two lovers that I thought twice and shall no doubt end up staying here. Rita feels the same and now visits them more regularly. Yesterday she told me that their marriage is certain.

'But who told you that they are getting married?'

'No one told me, I just put two and two together. When I said as much to Dona Carmo she was embarrassed, not wanting to confirm it and ashamed to deny it, that's what it is. But I changed the subject and spoke of something else. Only if they haven't said anything about it to her yet. . . .'

Some scruple made me hold my tongue, and I didn't tell her what Tristão himself had told me. It cost me nothing, so keeping up the pretence, I replied, 'Well, she's not marrying me, but according to you she's marrying someone else. So you admit you lost your bet?'

'I won't deny it. It's all in the hands of God.'

'You remember that day in the cemetery?'

'Yes, I remember. It was a year ago.'

I repeat, it cost me nothing to be discreet; it is a virtue for which I claim no merit. One day, when I feel I'm about to die, I'll read this page to Rita; and if I should die suddenly, let her read it and forgive me. It wasn't for lack of trust that I didn't tell her what I wrote just now.

Let her read it, and with it this other admission of my respect for her qualities as a sister and as a woman. Perhaps if we had lived together I might have discovered some trifling fault in her, or she in me, but separated as we are there is always a special delight in being together. From my reading of the classics, I remember an account in João de Barros of an African king's answer to the Portuguese sailors who asked him to give them, as his friends, a small plot of his land. The king replied that it was better that they should remain friends at a distance, because friends close were like a rock lying beside the sea, whose waves beat upon it with violence. It was a lively image, and if it didn't happen to be the one the African king used, it was nevertheless true.

Before going to bed I re-read what I had written at midday today and considered the last part too sceptical. My sister must forgive me.

I've just come back from Flamengo where I found Aguiar not too well. He was lying on a *chaise-longue* in the living room with the doors closed and in complete silence; just he and his wife were there. Tristão had gone to Botafogo; not that he didn't want to stay, but both of them insisted that he went as Fidelia might be alarmed if he didn't appear, and they sent their regards. Tristão gave way and left. I would have given way too, without much persuasion, which he probably didn't need either.

They didn't say so in exactly those terms, but what they said amounted to the same thing. They kept silent on the subject of the marriage.

Aguiar has a cold, but he'll soon be able to sweat that out of him. Despite this he refused to let me leave any earlier. Dona Carmo insisted that he go to bed, and I that I take my leave, but he declared that he didn't like to think of me returning to spend a miserable evening in a lonely house, and delayed me as long as he could. It wasn't too late when I left, and I had time to observe the lady of the house as she swung from one extreme to the other in her concern for her husband and her joy in her godson. Restless and worried, she would feel her husband's brow and pulse, and then, led on by him, talk about Fidelia or Tristão, and so the evening passed between one thing and the other, with the murmur of the sea and the chiming of the clock.

13 February

I sent round for news of Aguiar. He is better this morning, but won't risk going out. He's better though. He wrote inviting me to dinner with them. I replied that his illness was just an excuse to spend the day at home with his wife, and for that reason it is

137

impossible for me to go and witness this scene from Theocritus for myself.

In fact I can't go because I have to dine with the Belgian Chargé d'Affaires. To be honest I would prefer the Aguiars, not that the diplomat is a bore, just the opposite. But the old couple suit well with my old age, and with them I recover a little of my lost youth. The Belgian is a young man, but still a Belgian. What I mean is that being tired of hearing and speaking French, I found my own language fresher and more expressive, so that now I want to die with that on my lips and in my ears. My days are counted, and we can never recover even the shadow of what we lose.

'This scene from Theocritus', wrote Aguiar, in reply to my note declining his invitation, 'means something different from what it seems. Come and explain it to me tomorrow between soup and coffee, and you can also tell me about Belgium's secret designs. Tristão tells me he'll dine here too provided you come. You see what a pass that ungrateful rascal's come to when he'll only have dinner with us if we have visitors. If not he vanishes. Will you come, Counsellor?'

I replied to say that I'd go. In the last sentence of his note he makes a pretence of being hurt, but it is only a way of concealing his pleasure. In other words he knows the lad's absence is due to the love of two people who both love them and are loved by them too. I have no doubt that once dinner is over the first to send him off packing to Botafogo will be the Aguiars themselves.

15 February

No, they didn't pack Tristão off to Botafogo. I think they fully intended to but they were not given time. No sooner had we finished dinner than Fidelia and her uncle appeared. I guessed the lovers had arranged this beforehand.

It was an enjoyable evening for all. I amused myself observing the two of them. Not that they didn't try to pretend, she in particular, but in such circumstances no pretence will serve. The strength of their feelings upset their plans, and their eyes gave away their secrets. When they said little or nothing the silence revealed more than their words; bound up in each other, they were both of them in heaven. That is what it seemed to me. Nor did it seem unlikely that, inspired by heaven, they wished the Devil would take us all: me, the three old folk, Tristão's parents, the steamers, the trunks, the letters they expected, everything except a priest and some words of Latin – speedy words and speedier priest – to relieve them of their celibacy and their widowhood. And in this way they revealed all they knew of themselves.

They knew everything. It is incredible how two people who had never seen each other before, or who had met just casually, now knew each other perfectly and intimately. Their knowledge of one another was complete. If there was still some nook or corner to be discovered they uncovered it straight, each penetrating the other with a dazzling, ethereal light. What I have said may not seem to make sense, but it is not fantasy, it is only what I saw with my own eyes. And I envied them. I won't alter that remark: I envied them both, for in that transfusion the difference of sex disappeared to form one single entity.

16 February

Yesterday I forgot to mention one thing that happened the day before at the beginning of dinner at Flamengo. So here it is – I may need to refer to it tomorrow or later.

Our first mouthfuls of soup were drunk in a somewhat strained silence. Some letters (two) had arrived from Europe; Tristão read them rapidly at the window and didn't appear to like what he read. He began to eat distractedly and without pleasure. Naturally his godparents suspected something was wrong, but they didn't dare ask. They stole furtive glances at him, while I, not to cause them further anxiety, did not introduce any new topic but ate my food in silence. The tense moment did not last long and the rest of the meal passed off cheerfully. I have already noted what took place during the remainder of the evening.

If I had wanted to know what was in the letters I had only to be indiscreet or impolite and ask him privately. And I think Tristão would have told me, since he has taken to me more and more. He listens to me, talks to me, seeks me out and asks my advice and opinions. However, his ill humour was short-lived,

139

so it was probably nothing serious; he would have ended up confiding everything to his godparents as soon as they were alone, and certainly to his fiancée yesterday. They must have reached the stage of sharing their secrets by now.

18 February

Telegrams from Tristão's parents agreeing to everything and sending their blessing. Telegraphic style is concise, and that is how Tristão conveyed the news to me, word for word. Happiness makes one communicative. I shook his hand warmly, but he wanted an embrace. It was here at home, at two o'clock, just as I was on my way out. We left together, and I was obliged to hear three panegyrics, one of his parents, another of his godparents and the third (or rather the twentieth) of the lady of his heart.

'Dona Fidelia was delighted. She said she never had any doubt as to their answer, but the telegram shows that they wanted to reply immediately and not wait for the mail. Now we are waiting for their letters, but we can announce the engagement right away.'

On leaving the tram I was treated to a fourth panegyric, of his party leaders, who wrote saying that they are anxious to see him in the Chamber of Deputies. One went so far as to say that if Tristão abandons politics, he will do so too.

'He's exaggerating,' said Tristão, with a smile, 'but it shows that they want me there. It might also be a way of urging me to return quickly. The other merely said that my candidature is being submitted and that my election is assured.'

'Is that so? Congratulations.'

'Please, not just yet, and not in public. I haven't told any of this to my godparents. I told Dona Fidelia privately, and now you, but in the strictest confidence.'

Probably these were the two letters of the other day. But will he really go, or is he still undecided whether or not to yield to his wife should she wish to stay? No doubt the confidence he asked of me will eventually be explained one way or the other. . . .

Tristão and Fidelia's engagement is formally announced, not in the papers, which would have been a good thing, but only among the acquaintance of the two families. . . .

I like to see private matters published in the press; it is a good custom, making each one's personal life the concern of all. I've seen them not merely in print but actually immortalized by other means. The time will come when the photographer will be at the death bed to register the last moments, and if further intimacy were possible he'd be there too.

When Rita brought me the official news of the engagement I showed her my own letter communicating the fact and triumphantly demanded to know who had been right that time a year ago in the cemetery. She again agreed that it was I, but with the reservation that our bet had been that the widow would marry me, and she cited the wager between God and the Devil concerning Faust which I had read to her here at home from my volume of Goethe.

'No, you can't wriggle out of it, it was you who urged me to try, and made light of my age with flattering words, do you remember?'

She remembered, we smiled and began to talk about the young couple. I spoke well of both, she spoke ill of neither, but did so without warmth. Perhaps she was not pleased at seeing the widow marry, as if it were something reprehensible or newfangled. Not having re-married herself she felt that no one should marry a second time. Or else (forgive me dear sister, if you should read this one day) or else she now felt a twinge of remorse at not having done so too. . . . But no, that would be too much to suspect of such an excellent person.

That, in a few words, was the gist of our conversation. We did not speak of the date of the wedding, nor of their departure, that is if they are departing. Rita was not the one to repeat quips or jokes or spread rumours; her news had nothing malicious or unkind about it, just interesting things she had heard at the Aguiars'.

I've just arrived from town, where they confirmed that this morning Miranda had a cerebral congestion. Rita mentioned it just as she was leaving and I forgot to note it down. She was on the landing when she said she had heard the news on the tram from two strangers.

'And only now you tell me?' I said. She is right; life has its inalienable rights – first the living and their partners; the dead and their funerals can wait.

I did the same thing too: only now have I mentioned the man.

26 February

Miranda died yesterday at ten o'clock, and is being buried today at four. I think he has left his family well provided for. We got on well together though without being close friends. If I were to count up all the friends I have lost in one place and another it would come to several dozen. The papers say there will be no invitations to the funeral, so I'll go there without one.

10 p.m.

I went to Miranda's funeral. There would be no point in describing it if it weren't for what happened at the end. There were many people present and the usual display of grief. Even Cesaria seemed overcome, though I don't know whether she cried or not. Aguiar and Campos were there too, as well as other people I knew.

In the cemetery, after the last spadeful of earth had been thrown into the grave, I remembered to pay a visit to the family vault. I separated myself from the others and went there. I found it as well tended as usual and after a few minutes, seeing that people were still leaving, I walked over to the grave of Noronha, Fidelia's husband. I knew where it was though I hadn't been there before.

Now that his widow is about to bury him a second time I was curious to see it too, wondering to what extent I might apply to the dead man that verse of Shelley's which I had already quoted in respect of myself and the same beautiful lady: *I can*, and so forth. The tomb is austere, imposing and well kept, with two vases of fresh flowers, not planted, but picked and brought there that same morning. This convinced me that the flowers must be Fidelia's, and a gravedigger who was passing answered my question: 'A lady brings them from time to time. . . .'

The question was put so naturally that the gravedigger had no hesitation in answering, nor I in noting it here. Neither do I wish to conceal the thoughts that came to me then. The mourners who had accompanied Miranda's funeral had all gone. Another was arriving. Between one and the other I took a cab and came home. On the way I reflected that if it was true that Fidelia still took flowers to her husband's grave, either she was just keeping up the habit or she was still in love with him. You can make your own choice. I studied the question from both points of view, and was about to discover a third solution when we arrived at the front door. I got out, gave the cabby his usual tip, and went inside. I was tired. I undressed, wrote this note and will now go and have dinner. At the end of the evening, if possible, I'll write the third solution, if not, tomorrow. The third solution is what I wrote before, I don't remember the day. . . . Ah! it was the second anniversary of my return to Rio de Janeiro, when I imagined her contemplating her dead husband as if he were her future one, and making of both a single person in the present. I can't explain it any better because that is how I understand it myself, though incompletely. If ever Dona Cesaria got to know, she is capable of passing it on to Tristão himself, adding her touch of spite or malice, or both together for a change. . . . But not yet, she still hasn't got over the death of her brother-in-law. Everything passes away, even brothers-in-law.

Undated

Several days without writing anything. At first it was a touch of rheumatism in my finger, then visits, then lack of subject matter, in other words sheer laziness. I must shake off my laziness.

Last night I was at Fidelia's house, almost alone with her, for there were just her uncle, a colleague from the Court of Appeal and an elderly relative. Tristão had gone to Petropolis, and had been accompanied to the Prainha ferry by his godparents and by me who, seeing them in Rua da Quitanda, joined them in the cab at their invitation. They didn't say then the reason for his journey, but I already knew from the day before. It was to have a look at a house in which to spend their honeymoon. From that I concluded, I don't know why, that they would be staying here.

I can truly say that I was alone with her. When her uncle told me that his niece was missing her old friend – that's me – I thought he was lying and just wanted a partner for cards. I didn't go to play, which proved to be the right thing as the elderly relative went off to play *voltarete* with the two judges.

My relationship with Fidelia had reached the stage where I could ask her whether she was missing her fiancé. She replied affirmatively, but shyly, with a quick smile and a movement of her eyebrows. Tristão was the main topic of our conversation, I praising him warmly and sincerely, she answering without any show of pride, but rather with modesty and discretion, though in her heart she must have been pleased. She told me that he had received letters from his family confirming at greater length the brief messages they had sent. His mother's letter was full of tenderness, and she quoted some phrases used by her future mother-in-law. She went to fetch the letter so that I could read it too.

'Didn't he receive any letters from his political friends?'

'I think he did.'

I read the Paulista's letter and gave it high praise. It was certainly tender, though effusive, but a mother's tenderness is not bound by considerations of style. It was addressed to Fidelia herself.

Seeing that she was enjoying the conversation I did not ask for any music, but she went of her own accord to play the piano: a piece I don't know by which composer, but if Tristão didn't hear it in Petropolis it wasn't for lack of expression on the part of the pianist. Eternity is even further off, and there she had already dispatched a portion of her heart. The great advantage of music is that it speaks both to the dead and to the absent.

144

Saturday

Fidelia seems more reserved now after those first few confidences, which is only natural. When I asked her for news of Tristão she replied that she hadn't received any, and changed the subject. Then when I mentioned Dona Carmo's new-found happiness she told me how miserable the old lady had been once when thinking of her godson's return, and mentioned her own suggestion that Dona Carmo should go with him. The reply was that she would have to be separated from her husband, and this she couldn't do.

'You see the danger of sharing your heart between two people. As a young man I never did, and much less would I do so now I'm old.'

On this subject (which had no clear meaning or special intention) we said things which are not worthy of note here. What she said was spoken wittily and was probably correct, but we avoided the principal subject, that closest to her heart. I found enjoyment in the appreciation of her mind and her person, the former being no less interesting than the latter. Losing nothing of the discretion that so becomes her, Fidelia speaks her mind with no false modesty, full of assurance, and for all this I thank her here.

9 March

Tristão has returned from Petropolis. He has rented a house in Vestefália by arrangement with Judge Josino, who is leaving it for some time and going with his family to the south. He gave him a contract for three months. Dona Carmo and Fidelia are going up to see it this week. They are much more together nowadays, both in the house and out of doors, which is natural since they are that much closer. I walk with them too whenever I meet them, and also listen to what they have to say.

'So you see, my dear sister,' I said to Rita, telling her about these things at Andaraí, 'what is the fate of a respectable old retired diplomat, admittedly without the burdens of office, but also without hopes of promotion.'

Rita understood and almost took me to task, but preferred to say with words of comfort and affection that at least my thoughts had not strayed to the cemetery. This allusion to the visit we paid to the family vault more than a year ago almost induced me to confess the paternal feelings that Fidelia sometimes arouses in me, but I held back in time. More than likely Rita would tell me, as she once did, that they were the excuses of a bad debtor. She loves to pull people's legs, but never so as to cause rancour, especially with me, who worship her. It comes down to this, that there are things which ought to be written down and not spoken about, which is what I am now doing with respect to this new kind of feeling I have towards Fidelia.

13 March

There is nothing like the passion of love to give originality to what is commonplace and novelty to what is dying of old age. Such are these two lovers, whom I never tire of listening to, so fascinating I find them. The drama of love, apparently created by the serpent's perfidy and man's disobedience, has not yet ceased to provoke floods on this earth. From time to time some poet sings its praises amid the tears of the spectators; nothing more than that. The drama is an everyday one; it exists in every form and is as new as the sun, which itself is old.

20 March

Dona Carmo has taken it upon herself to decorate the house of the engaged couple. I learned this from Campos, who arrived from Petropolis, where he left the house looking 'a treat' as the result of her arrangement of the furniture and decorations, some of these the work of her own hands.

'What, already?' I asked.

'Already. Dona Carmo works fast, and just now with extraordinary dedication; she has even given them some things she made herself. Talk to Aguiar, he'll tell you the same thing, and Tristão too, not to mention Fidelia.'

Rita, without seeing anything, agrees it must be so, that is what she said to me. Dona Cesaria, on the other hand, who like her has seen nothing, is inclined to believe that the décor is lacking in harmony.

'It might not be,' I ventured to say.

146

'I'm not saying that Dona Carmo isn't capable of making a good job of it, but so hastily, in such a rush, it's not likely. In any case her taste is not all that reliable; she has a certain amount, but she lacks polish. The young couple as well; he seems to be a show-off. . . .'

I wanted to speak up for the three, but the certainty that she has no higher opinion of me held me back, and I merely said that I had never seen her in such high spirits. I went further, and praised her eyes. As she was then passing her fingers over her eyebrows I praised her hand too, and would have passed on to her feet, had she shown me her feet, but she showed me nothing more.

21 March

Let me explain what I said yesterday. It wasn't fear that led me to admire Dona Cesaria's high spirits, her eyes, her hands, and by implication the rest of her person. I have already mentioned some of her good qualities. It happens, however, that this lady's love of spreading scandal is not lessened by any compliments she receives, and no matter how beautiful I find her teeth, she will be only too ready to sink them into my back whenever it suits her. No, I praised her not to remove her sting but to amuse myself, and rest of the evening I didn't spend too badly. I was at her house, where her sister with her recent widowhood threw a gloom over everything. Dona Cesaria's words scattered both poison and honey, but she interchanged and complemented them with such skill that occasionally one seemed the other and both seemed the same thing.

22 March

The following observation is a short one, and if it weren't it would be better to keep it for tomorrow or later this evening when I go to bed. But it is short.

Short and to the point. Tristão may end up throwing his political career overboard. From what I heard and wrote last year about his early life, he was not quick to make up his mind; he changed his inclinations, he changed his preferences. His career was going to be one thing and he ended up becoming a doctor and a politician, and when he comes on a holiday and business trip he ends up getting married. As far as the last part is concerned it is not surprising, for destiny had decreed him a fortunate encounter; the fellow would accept handcuffs if they were pretty enough, and here they are beautiful.

He talks less of parties and elections and no longer tells me what the leaders have written to him. With me, at least, he only speaks of Fidelia, and I doubt he is any more forthcoming with others, remaining silent about his political ambitions in the near and distant future. No, he is all Fidelia, and he may well send his parliamentary seat to the Devil if his bride asks him to. Could he be fickle, always enslaved by the latest attraction? It may be, and if so, so much the better for the Aguiars. If that is what happens I'll read this page to the old couple, and with this last line in it too.

25 March

As today is the anniversary of the Constitution I was thinking of going to pay my respects to the Emperor, but Tristão's visit made me give up the idea. I remained chatting with him about a thousand different things, then we went for a walk and came home.

He couldn't accept my invitation to stay for dinner as he was going to dine with her. Naturally we spoke of her occasionally, he enthusiastically, I sympathetically. It is probably true that I spoke less than he did, but I am just a friend of them both and my preference, as always, is to listen.

Another subject we discussed, though less than her, was politics, not Brazilian or Portuguese but that of other countries. Tristão attended the Commune in France, and it seems that outside England he is conservative; when there he is liberal, while in Italy he remains staunchly Latin. With his wide interests, his inquiring mind seeks out and absorbs everything. One thing I noted is that wherever he is, he has an obsession for politics, and is seemingly born and bred for the political life. A further thing is that there is no hatred in him; he would be incapable of persecuting his enemies. In short, he's a fine lad, as I am never tired of writing, and would not refrain from saying so now that he's about to marry. All bridegrooms are fine lads.

Or bene, Tristão and Fidelia's wedding has been fixed for May 15th. This had been secretly arranged between them so that the papers in Lisbon should be ready in time. The ones here are being prepared.

It was Dona Carmo herself who gave me the news today before I received it by letter, seeing that both are friends of mine and that the three or four of us are so much together, but in fact she spoke for herself.

'A great dream of mine is being realized, Counsellor,' she said. 'At last I shall have them both with me. I am hoping to find a house for them here in Flamengo. She told me once that she felt like my daughter. . . .'

'That was at your silver wedding party, wasn't it?'

'You heard her?'

'No, I didn't hear her, but I saw what she did, which amounts to the same thing. Remember that I was sitting beside you, and she next to your husband, so we were close together. I don't forget such things.'

'That's right. I was so happy I could never have imagined that greater happiness was to come.'

To steer the conversation in a different direction I repeated that I never forgot anything, and told her of various incidents I remember vividly, but all of them when I was a young man. Nowadays a great deal escapes me, I confuse things and get them mixed up. But at least I succeeded in changing the course of our conversation, which was what I wanted so as not to spoil the old lady's happiness by any indiscreet question about politics. I hadn't counted on her bringing the subject up, as she did, saying that Tristão no longer talks to her about politics, and that he receives fewer letters, or only uninteresting ones which he doesn't show to anyone, putting them in his pocket or skimming through them quickly. His mother wrote to him a short time ago.

'She sent me a message that I was trying to steal her son, and threatened to come and fetch him with a gunboat. I sent her a joking letter in reply.'

Just then Dona Cesaria came into the room and was given

the news of the date of the wedding. She had heard rumours of it and had come to find out if they were true. She showed such kindly interest that it in part made up for the ill she had spoken of Dona Carmo, and in a way confirmed views I had once held (I don't know whether I wrote them down) about the justice of this world. God here triumphed over the Devil with such a sweet, tender smile that one forgot the existence of his sooty counterpart. On the other hand, the lady's husband would, in my opinion, be incapable of such a contrast – he lacks the disposition and principally the manners. He's the type that would thank you for telling him that he had won first prize in the lottery by giving you a kick. He doesn't know how to be happy, even when it costs him nothing. I don't know whether I am explaining myself clearly, but at any rate that is what I feel. Reflecting on this and other matters helped to pass the time, and by eleven o'clock I was back home.

Before going to bed it occurred to me that it is true that Tristão no longer talks to me about politics, nor does he quote from the letters he receives, so maybe he really hasn't been receiving many. If I were a poet I'd end up composing a hymn to the god of love, but since I'm not it will have to be in prose: 'Love, great among political parties, thou art the strongest party in the world. . . .' I'll read this page to the young couple after they are married.

4 April

This was one thing I hadn't bargained for. Tristão came to ask me to be best man at his wedding. I couldn't refuse, so I accepted, though I wasn't keen. There's Aguiar, or Campos, but after all I want to do my best to make everyone happy. He gave me further details: the wedding will be a simple one, between eleven o'clock and midday, family lunch at Flamengo, after which a few of us will escort the two of them to Prainha, where they will embark for Petropolis. The details were unnecessary, but one must always listen with full attention to a man in love.

'Do you know what Dona Fidelia has just written to tell me?' asked Aguiar. 'That she wants the bank to be responsible for selling Santa-Pia.'

'I seem to remember hearing about that. . . .'

'Yes, it was some time ago, but it was just a vague idea. Now I see that it wasn't. . . .'

'Are the freed slaves still working there?'

'Yes, but they say it is only on her account.'

I don't remember whether I made any comment on freedom and slavery, but it is possible, I having no interest whatever in whether Santa-Pia fazenda is sold or not. My particular interest is in the *fazendeira*, that *fazendeira* who lives in the city and is to be married in the city. The marriage is already much commented on, with a great deal of surprise and probably not a little envy. There are even those who ask after Noronha. Where's Noronha? What became of Noronha?

Not many ask – though more women than men – either because they were upset by Fidelia's tears, or because they are more interested in Tristão, or because they cannot deny that the widow is beautiful. So great is their curiosity that it may be that all three reasons get lumped together. Nevertheless the question gets asked, and the answer goes something like this: 'Ah, my friend, if I were to inquire what happens to the dead I should pass through the infinite to end up in eternity.'

It's cleverly put, but it's not right, mainly because it's not true. The dead end up in the cemetery, where, with flowers and memories, they receive the affection of the living. This will happen to Fidelia herself when she goes there, as it has happened to Noronha, who is already there. The vital thing is that this link is not really broken, and that the law of life does not allow what lived and died to be destroyed. I believe in Fidelia's two loves, even to the extent of believing that the two combine, one being a continuation of the other.

When I was active in the diplomatic corps I would not have believed in such things, I was uneasy and suspicious. But if I retired it was to be able to have faith in the sincerity of others. Let those who are still active keep their suspicions.

Santa-Pia is no longer for sale, not for lack of buyers, just the opposite. In five days two appeared who know the fazenda, and only the first objected to the price. But it is not for sale, that is what I was told this morning. I assumed that Tristão and Fidelia would be making their home there which, if true, would be even more surprising.

What I heard later is that Tristão, learning of Fidelia's intentions, thought up a new scheme, which he put to her. Not in clear, direct terms, but by suggestion. Since the freed slaves only continue working out of love for their young mistress, what is there to stop her taking the fazenda and handing it over to her former slaves? Let them work it for themselves. He did not put it in so many words, but in a deliberately casual way so that his suggestion did not seem over-generous. That is how Fidelia herself interpreted it, as she told Dona Carmo, who passed it on to me.

'Tristão is as capable of possessing the good intention as he is of disguising it,' the old lady added, 'but I also feel that his main motive was to remove any suspicion that he was marrying out of self-interest. However that may be, it appears that is what they are going to do.'

'And to think that we still have critics arguing about romantics and naturalists!'

Dona Carmo did not seem to find my remark amusing, and I myself find it neither amusing nor meaningful. I applauded the change of plan, the new one seeming to me a good one. If they don't intend to live on the fazenda and don't need the money from its sale, the best thing is to give it to the freed slaves. Will these be able to manage it together to justify their young mistress's generosity? That is another question, but I am not bothered whether I see it resolved or not: there are plenty of other things in this world far more interesting.

When I spoke to Tristão about the donation of Santa-Pia he told me nothing about any secret motives, merely saying that Fidelia is going to sign the document tomorrow or the day after. We

were having coffee in the Carceler restaurant. He also said that
he has received more letters from Lisbon, two of them from party
leaders, urging him to return. I wanted to find out if he is going
to respond to their urging, but from the way he contemplated the
smoke rising from his cigar he seemed to be seeing only his bride,
the altar and their future happiness. I dared not break the spell.

On leaving the Carceler he said he was going to do some
shopping; it is possibly a present for his fiancée, but he did not
say what it was or who it was for. He did speak of his godmother
and of her friendship for him, to which I replied, in confirmation,
'I can assure you that it is sincere.'

'Sincere, and of long-standing.'

He then told me what I already knew, incidents from his
childhood and adolescence, and entertained me with this while
we walked on and the minutes slowly passed. I feel he's a
good sort and a good friend. The age at which he left here
and the time he has lived in Portugal make his pronunciation
a mixture of Rio and Lisbon, but it is not disagreeable, just the
opposite. We said goodbye outside a goldsmith's. It must be a
jewel.

28 April

Santa-Pia has been made over to the freed slaves, who will
probably receive it with dancing and weeping. But maybe this
new, or rather first responsibility . . .

6 May

The Aguiars look worried. Tristão received more letters and some
newspapers from Lisbon and read them slowly to himself, first
looking cheerful, then frowning. What he read in the papers
were some passages marked in blue pencil and black ink, none of
which he showed to his godparents. Instead he took them to his
bedroom, where neither of them saw fit to ask to see them. They
made no comment, and he remained lost in his own reflections;
so passed the remainder of the afternoon. After dinner they went
to Botafogo.

There the gloom was dissipated, for whenever Tristão and
Fidelia met it was like a new dawn for both. The Aguiars forgot

their worries and by the end of the evening the family was as light hearted as ever.

I wasn't there, but I heard of this from Rita, who chatted to Dona Carmo and then came to tell me all about it 'as to one whose lips are sealed', as she said. I accepted her confidences, thanked her for her good opinion, and end with this final thought. Indeed, Tristão is the kind of man whom politics could carry away with no effort, and Fidelia could retain here without difficulty.

8 May

Tristão wants to be married by Father Bessa and has already asked him. The priest, barely able to hear his request, agreed and thanked him, quite overcome with pleasure. There is something particularly fitting in having the marriage blessing given by the same priest who baptized him, which is no doubt what Tristão had in mind, but probably his principal aim was simply to give him pleasure. That obscure priest, tucked away there in Formosa, will mount the steps of Gloria Church (where the wedding is to take place) to give his blessing to the marriage of two handsome and personable young people. Aguiar told me that the priest looks as if it were he who was the bridegroom.

'And remember, Counsellor,' he said, giving me a piece of news that was already several days old, 'remember that when Tristão gave him a present of a new cassock he was very embarrassed because it made him realize just how threadbare his old one was. Now you can't imagine how openly delighted he is. I think it is the chance to perform his spiritual and sacramental duties once more; he hasn't married anyone for years.'

15 May

Married at last. I have just returned from Prainha, where I went to see them off on the Petropolis ferry. The wedding was on the dot of midday, in Gloria Church, with few people but a great deal of activity. Fidelia, looking very serious, wore a dark, high-necked dress with sleeves buttoned at the wrists with garnets. Dona Carmo, despite her sober dress, was wreathed in smiles, as was her husband. Tristão looked radiant. As we mounted the steps I exchanged a glance with Rita and I think we both smiled; I don't

154

know about her, but with me it was the memory of that day in the cemetery and of what she told me about Noronha's widow. And here we were with her at her second wedding. Such was the will of Destiny. I call it that to give it the name I am accustomed to from my reading, and to be honest, I like it. It gives the idea of something fixed and definite. After all it rhymes well enough with *divinity*, and spares me the trouble of philosophical conjectures.

In the church the onlookers from the neighbourhood, mainly women, were all eyes as they gazed at the bridal couple in their progress from the door to the high altar. To describe the agitation, the whispers, the bent heads would be to fill this sheet to no purpose. It would be more interesting to know what was said of her first wedding and its joys, of the widow and her sorrows, and of all the other phases of this eternal moon of creation.

When the ceremony was over and Father Bessa left the altar, Dona Carmo was overcome with emotion. I saw the hug she gave to each in turn, and then together. Tristão kissed her hand, Fidelia too, both of them moved, and she more so than them; she finally sealed everything with two motherly kisses. At one in the afternoon we were back at Flamengo, and shortly afterwards had lunch. Just now I am too tired to describe everything that happened before, during and after the meal, up to the time when we accompanied the newly-weds to Prainha. Everything went off as expected, except for the very special attention the four of them paid to me. Amongst those present I haven't mentioned Campos, who was by no means the least delighted person there, even though Tristão is carrying off his niece, who has been half wife, half daughter to him because of the order she maintained in his house ever since she went to live with him. Neither have I mentioned his son, her cousin. The remainder were just a few close friends.

There was one incident, so timely that it seemed to be deliberate. In the middle of lunch there arrived a telegram for Tristão from Lisbon, with just three words, two names and the date: 'God bless you.' His parents had been informed by letter that the wedding was today and wished to send their blessings by cable. Tristão read the words to himself, then out loud for all to hear, and then the telegram was passed round the table.

Naturally the newly-weds clasped each other's hands, and Dona Carmo expressed the real mother's wishes in the tender looks of the adopted mother. I could not but be affected by all that emotion, not that I shared it, but it made me feel good. I am not much longer for this world, but it is not a bad thing to set out having one's eyes fixed on those one leaves behind.

So it was quite easy for me to propose the health of the bride and groom, which I did discreetly, including the Aguiars in the toast, for which they were grateful. When we got back from Prainha, Rita told me that my speech was delightful. I replied that it would have been more appropriate had I just emended those lines of Bernardim Ribeiro: 'Widow and bride took me from my parents' house to far-off lands. . . .'* But apart from awakening memories of her first husband, the far-off lands might be extended beyond Petropolis and strike a discordant note in such a happy gathering.

'It was better to keep to my delightful speech,' I concluded, modestly.

26 May

These last few days I have been out only to visit the Aguiars, who seem to grow fonder of me every day. They are happy, exchanging letters with their two adopted children. These will be coming down next week, but will return the same day, the purpose of their visit being just to greet the old couple.

In Petropolis they have had rain, but they have had fine days too, and Fidelia makes her impressions of both sound interesting, no doubt the result of being a newly married bride. One's own heart gives life to external things, both the bitter and the sweet as the case may be, and Fidelia's letters could not be sweeter. Dona Carmo showed me the girl's last letter, written in a small, compact hand, narrowly spaced. The tenderness she expresses does not outrun her discretion, neither does the latter diminish the former. At the end of the letter Fidelia suggests the possibility of all four of them going to Europe, or just the three if Aguiar is unable to leave the bank. The old lady is going to reply that just now she is not able to.

---

* The original is 'Child and maiden'.

'Neither now nor ever,' she said, folding the letter. 'I'm tired and frail, Counsellor, and my health is not good. This nonsense of travelling around is not for me.'

'But travelling is good for your health and restores your strength,' I suggested.

'It may be so, but for those who are younger. At my age it is impossible.'

There was a pause during which Aguiar glanced at his wife, she at him and I at both alternately. Then a neighbour came in and we talked of other matters.

Thursday

Tristão and Fidelia came down today and Aguiar went to meet them at Prainha. From there they went to have lunch at Flamengo, where Dona Carmo was waiting for the newly-weds and embraced them with a full heart. Aguiar arranged to go from the bank to Prainha when the afternoon ferry left for Petropolis.

This is what the old couple told me that evening, adding that Dona Carmo and the young people spent the delightfullest day possible. This wasn't the actual adjective she used because as I have already mentioned Dona Carmo is not given to exaggeration. But what she said amounted to that.

The three of them talked of various things, of Petropolis, music and painting, and the young couple played the piano. Shortly afterwards they went for a walk together along the beach. It was there that Fidelia returned to the idea she had suggested in her letter, that they should make a journey to Europe – an idea which Dona Carmo had rejected, alleging she was too tired and frail. Then Fidelia explained the trip she had in mind: in the first place a short stay in Lisbon to see Tristão's mother, then on to Paris and, if there was time, Italy. They would leave in August or September and in December they would be back.

'It's not the time, my child,' replied Dona Carmo. 'Long or short, once there I would go through with it to the end, but this old body of mine is tired. In any case, if Aguiar doesn't go who would look after him?'

'He can come too,' said Tristão.

'This year he can't.'

157

They continued talking as they walked along the beach, where the advance and retreat of the waves seemed to be beckoning them to set forth and sail until they reached the 'port of the renowned Ulysseia',* as the poet says. It occurred to Dona Carmo to ask them why they didn't put off the journey until next year, when Aguiar could go too, but they did not answer.

'I would have refused anyway,' said Aguiar that evening when they were telling me this. 'I told them so at Prainha when I went to see them off on the ferry. And I wouldn't leave Carmo either.'

11 June

Today I met the newly-weds for the first time. It was a chance meeting at two o'clock in the afternoon in Rua do Ouvidor, where they had gone to do some shopping. I was glad to hear what they had to say, and even more to see Fidelia. The elegance with which she gave her arm to her husband and stepped lightly along the street was more pronounced than before her marriage. The result of marriage and happiness. They walked along talking, listening and stopping in front of the shop windows.

They will be returning to Rio on the 20th of this month and will leave for Lisbon at the beginning of August. Then on to other places.

'Why don't you come too, Counsellor?' asked Tristão.

'After all the travelling I've done? I'm only just beginning to accustom myself to *our* country again.'

I stress this *our* because I spoke the word with a certain emphasis, but I don't think he even heard it. He was gazing at his wife as if anticipating the pleasures of the journey they were to make, then they went on their way down the street with the same leisurely elegance.

25 June

Campos and Aguiar each wanted the young couple to stay in his house, alleging that it would only be for a few days since they were nearly ready to embark. Tristão and Fidelia refused, and went to the Hotel dos Estrangeiros. They gave the same excuse that it was

---

* i.e., Lisbon. The reference is to the epic poem *Os Lusíadas* by Camões.

for so few days, which I think was true, but the main reason was not to give preference to one or the other.

'We'll spend these last few days alternating between the two houses,' suggested Tristão.

'No, don't do that,' said Campos. 'We'll spend them all at Flamengo.'

This was both natural and polite, he being single and Aguiar married. So that is what they have been doing since the 20th, which is when the two came down from Petropolis. I met them there yesterday, St John's Day.

I won't say what took place there or I shall be tempted to describe everything, which was a great deal. All four of them looked happy. Dona Carmo seemed as if trying to hide her sadness at the forthcoming journey, or to moderate it, by the idea of their return, which she referred to frequently and at every opportunity as if to emphasize this obligation. The hours slipped by quickly in this manner. When they left I went with them as far as the hotel; from there Campos carried on to Botafogo and I came home to Catete.

29 June

My last visit was on St John's Night. Today is St Peter's, so I'll go along to Flamengo again and all being well we'll have another chat about old times.

30 June

I went to the Aguiars', where we talked neither about the past, nor the present, but only about the future. At the end of the evening I noticed that everyone was talking except the newly-weds, who, after a few desultory words, simply whispered and muttered among themselves. From time to time they put in an occasional word only to relapse once more into complete silence. They played the piano, then went to stand together in a corner of the window. Left to ourselves, we four old people – Campos and the three of us – made plans for the future.

Occasionally Dona Carmo would throw them a worried look, as if asking them what part they were to play in the future that she and we were planning, but the fear of interrupting their happiness made her hold her tongue, and the sweet old lady contented herself with gazing at them with loving eyes.

Over tea we all of us joined in the conversation, and Tristão spoke about Lisbon, political matters and amusements.

On the way home a thought occurred to me, an indiscreet one which fortunately I did not mention to anyone, and I am tempted not even to consign to my journal. It was to know whether Fidelia, after her marriage, has been back to the cemetery. Perhaps she has, perhaps she hasn't. I shan't censure her if she hasn't, for the human heart is too small to accommodate two great loves. If she has, I shall not blame her, just the opposite. The dead are perfectly capable of defying the living without defeating them entirely.

Undated

Today was the Aguiars' last at-home and I went there to say goodbye to the young couple, who sail the day after tomorrow. There were a lot of people, among whom were Faria and Dona Cesaria, and Miranda's widow, still disconsolate. It was not a cheerful gathering, just the opposite, for all the guests accommodated themselves to the atmosphere of the house, which was gloomy. Even Fidelia seemed jaded as she sat beside Dona Carmo, and once Rita heard her say to her companion, 'Why don't you come with us, Dona Carmo? There's still time to buy tickets, and if there aren't any left Tristão will postpone the trip and we'll all go on the next boat.'

Dona Carmo said no, she felt too tired and run down.

'But travelling isn't tiring, and once there you'll gain new life.'

Rita added her voice to the girl's, both of them trying to convince her, but it was no use. Her final argument was that of leaving her husband on his own; it was the old one but it was decisive. Rita noted that the two women were genuinely upset, but whereas Dona Carmo tried to put a brave face on it, Fidelia was unable to hide her disappointment.

'And you know something, I still think she's capable of cancelling the trip. . . .'

It was in the dark, coming from the beach, and for this reason Rita could not see my gesture of incredulity, but no doubt she guessed it for she amended her words: 'No, I won't say she'd

160

cancel it, but she'd give a lot never to have agreed to travel.'
She repeated what Fidelia said about Dona Carmo, calling her
good-hearted and saintly, 'The saintly Senhora Aguiar.'

I must say that I came away in an ill humour, and would have
preferred not to have gone or to have left early. Tristão is having
lunch with me tomorrow.

Eve of embarkation

Tristão kept his promise and came for lunch; it was half-past
eleven. He was downcast and uncommunicative, which meant
that we spoke very little. There being no better subject than
the silence itself I said that I understood his feelings at leaving
here, the country, the people, and particularly the two people
who loved him so much. It was a good opportunity to say
complimentary things about the old couple, or rather to repeat
them as I had said the same things many times before. At the
same time I hoped to discover his plans for the future, where his
journey would take him and how soon he intended to return with
his beautiful wife. He said nothing, merely nodding his head and
withdrawing into his original complete silence. I don't think he
heard the half of what I said.

After lunch, while we were smoking, he once again gave me the
address of his house in Lisbon and the name of the newspaper he
was writing for; it seemed he was about to add something else,
but he changed his mind and withdrew once more into silence.
Out of respect for his low spirits I concentrated my attention on
my cigar. Tristão finally rose to leave.

'Shall we meet again?' he asked.

'I'm going to the Pharoux quay. I'll maybe go on board too.'

'Till tomorrow, then. Let me know what we can do for you.'

I went with him to the stairs, and he began to go down slowly
after shaking my hand vigorously. Half-way down he stopped
and came up again.

'Look, Counsellor, Fidelia and I did all we could to persuade
the old folks to come with us. They can't come: she says she
is too tired, he won't leave her on her own and they are both
expecting us to return.'

'Then return quickly,' I said.

With an enigmatic look Tristão walked past me into the living room. I followed him.

'Counsellor, I'm going to let you into a secret which I have not told and do not intend to tell to anyone else. I count on your discretion.'

I gave a gesture of assent, whereupon he took a coloured paper from his trouser pocket, opened it and gave it to me to read. It was a telegram from his father, dated the previous day and informing him that the election would take place in a week's time.

We looked at each other without speaking, he seemingly clenching his teeth. After a few seconds he went on, 'My election is assured. I gathered that from previous letters, but I didn't think it would be so soon.'

I handed him back the telegram, and without letting me speak, he continued: 'I wanted them to come with us. On board ship I could have explained whatever was necessary, and the rest could have been arranged between the two women – or the three, if we include my mother. But it was no use; they'll wait for our return.'

I felt like saying that it would be like waiting for a dead man's shoes, but I brushed aside the proverb and thought of something else. However, as he remained silent I hesitated to speak, but after a moment he completed his thought, adding, 'I have opened my heart to you so that one day someone who is close to us all will testify that I did everything I could so as not to be separated from those whom I look upon almost as my own father and mother. But it was all to no avail. What more could I do, Counsellor? In life the unexpected happens, and we are pulled one way and the other. . . .'

I don't know what I answered. Another idea came to me, but which I did not mention, not wishing to be indiscreet. It was to ask if Fidelia knew of the telegram. He told me that he had not shown it to anyone, but obviously his wife was part of himself and was not to be included in the silence he maintained with others.

18 July

I have just returned from the ship, where with Aguiar, Campos and other friends I went to see the young couple off. Dona Carmo went as far as the quayside; she was overcome, and stayed there drying her eyes. She remained to watch the launch which took us out to wave goodbye with her handkerchief. Before long she was lost to sight.

Fidelia looked miserable, but the sea would soon drive away her gloom, and then there was a new country waiting to receive her, a new world opening up. As I stood on the deck I recalled the cemetery, the grave, her standing there with her hands folded, and all the rest of it. Tristão said goodbye to Aguiar with words of affection and gratitude and a message for Dona Carmo, while he begged me not to forget his godparents but to visit them and comfort them. I promised I would. Then we re-boarded the launch and drew away from the ship.

I have embarked and disembarked so many times that I ought to be used to it. But I'm not, though I can't say the parting meant much to me; my eyes were fixed on old Aguiar and my thoughts on Dona Carmo. Campos was miserable at parting from his niece, but she had extracted a last-minute promise from him that he would go to visit them next year, he not realizing that her request contradicted her own promise to return to Rio de Janeiro at the end of the year.

We parted on the quayside. Aguiar went to the bank, while I came home to write this. At night I'll call in at Flamengo so as to keep my promise to Tristão and Fidelia right away.

I can't finish this page without saying that just now the image of Fidelia appeared before my eyes exactly as I had left her on board ship, but without her tears. She sat down on the sofa and we remained gazing at each other, she exuding charm, I giving the lie to Shelley with all my remaining sexagenarian strength. Enough of that! I'd better think of going round to see the old couple soon.

10 p.m.

I've just come back from Flamengo. I would have stayed longer but the leave-taking had tired them and they needed to rest. Campos went too and we left together early, at half-past nine. We didn't speak of those at sea.

A steamer arrived from Europe bringing letters from Lisbon and news of political events. The letters are full of tender sentiments and the news of interest; they only arrived last night. In the street Aguiar had told me what was in the letters, which were from Tristão and Fidelia and from Tristão's mother to Dona Carmo. I went to Flamengo to see them. His mother's was full of praise for her daughter-in-law: she said she found her prettier than her portrait and the sweetest girl in the world. Those were her very words, and for a mother-in-law I didn't find them too inappropriate. I said as much to Dona Carmo, who smiled her agreement with a kind of morbid tenderness. We were just the three of us, and we missed the others badly.

A little later Campos arrived looking bewildered, and on seeing me seemed to want to speak to me in private. Alone together in a corner of the room he told me that Tristão had written to say that on disembarking in Lisbon he found himself already elected deputy, and had asked him to pass this news on to the Aguiars as he thought fit; he had not written to them about it so as not to give them a shock. What did I think?

'If they have to be told everything,' I replied, 'it is best to get it over with. We can put it to them tactfully now.'

'I agree.'

'I'll make up some story. . . .'

I did my best. I spoke of the shock the lad received on disembarking to find himself already elected deputy and being congratulated by his parents and party friends. I might have gone on to say that Tristão's first impulse was to reject it and return to Santa-Pia, but that the party, the leaders, his parents. . . . But I didn't carry it to that length; the lie would have been too much of a lie. In any case there was no time. The old couple were thunderstruck, she weeping silent tears, he attempting to dry her eyes.

That is how things worked out, the lie and its consequences. The two made an effort to revive their spirits, while I employed a variety of reflections and metaphors to convince them that, once they were aware of the grief their news had caused here, the two would be back before the end of the year or the beginning of the next.

Dona Carmo seemed not to hear me, neither did he. They were gazing out into the distance to where this life ends and everything hastens to a close. Aguiar even took the letter which Campos showed him and read for himself Tristão's words, hurtful enough in themselves, not counting the tone the author had deliberately given them. Dona Carmo made a sign, wanting to see it, but he put it in his pocket. The old lady didn't insist. Campos and I left shortly afterwards.

30 August

Walking by the beach (I forgot to note this yesterday), walking by the beach and talking of the inverted orphanhood in which the two old folk were left, I said to Campos, thinking of the dead husband, 'Judge, if the dead go quickly, the old do so even more quickly. Long live youth!'

Campos didn't completely understand me at first. So I had to explain that I was alluding to the dead husband and to the two old people the young ones had left, and I ended up declaring that the young have the right to live and to love, and to leave the dead and the aged behind them with no regrets. He didn't agree – which shows that even then he didn't fully understand me.

Undated

I hadn't been to Flamengo for six or seven days, so this afternoon I remembered to call in on my way home. I walked there and, finding the garden gate open, went in and then stopped.

There they are, I said to myself.

Inside, at the entrance to the porch, I could see the old couple sitting down gazing at each other. Aguiar was leaning against the right doorpost with his hands on his knees. Dona Carmo, on the left, had her arms folded on her lap. I debated for a moment whether to go on or turn back, and stood there hesitating for a few seconds before retreating on tiptoe. As I passed through the gate into the street I saw on their faces and in their attitude an expression which I find it impossible to describe. This is what it seemed to me: they were trying to smile, but barely succeeded in comforting each other. Memories were their only consolation.